Save the Tomatoes for Packy

SAVE THE TOMATOES FOR PACKY

A NOVEL

DANIEL A. DOHERTY, JR.

Save the Tomatoes for Packy

A novel

Daniel A. Doherty, Jr.

ZIMBELL HOUSE
PUBLISHING
UNION LAKE, MICHIGAN

For permission requests, write to the publisher
"Attention: Permissions Coordinator"
Zimbell House Publishing
PO Box 1172
Union Lake, Michigan 48387
mail to: info@zimbellhousepublishing.com

© 2020 Daniel A. Doherty, Jr.

Published in the United States by Zimbell House Publishing
http://www.ZimbellHousePublishing.com
All Rights Reserved

Hardcover ISBN: 978-1-64390-139-8
Trade Paper ISBN: 978-1-64390-140-4
.mobi ISBN: 978-1-64390-141-1
ePub ISBN: 978-1-64390-142-8
Large Print ISBN: 978-1-64390-143-5
Library of Congress Control Number: 2020900053

First Edition: April 2020
10 9 8 7 6 5 4 3 2 1

ZIMBELL HOUSE PUBLISHING
UNION LAKE

Dedication

This book is dedicated to Kathy. She will always be my inspiration to try to be a better man. And to Joe and Bobby, who left parts of their bodies and minds in a strange land and have earned the mercy of the Lord.

Contents

Chapter 1

The Final Journey

He always got a little nervous, even now, when the plane bounced around in the air. *Ironic,* he thought, after all these years, and the adventures leading up to this flight, that he was jittery. The turbulence soon ended, and Paul looked out of the window, turned off the jet stream nozzle of air above him, and wondered what the cemetery would look like. In his mind, the picture was remarkably clear, considering that he had never been to this graveyard, or even to this section of New York State. It was winter, and the snows that had fallen in this part of the country were marbled with dirt, and assorted detritus pushed up from the plows. The gravestones would be all different heights, some tilted or toppled. There would be tattered American flags on some, plastic flowers on others, but for the most part, it would be a settled community with new neighbors depicted by fresh dirt and new depressions.

Paul wasn't a handsome man in the magazine model sense. He was tall, thin, and still had all his hair at the age of fifty-nine, with little gray. Even though his buddies constantly chided him about dyeing his hair, he didn't. He gave up defending himself on that point, seriously considering coloring his hair gray.

They probably don't make gray hair coloring, though. Wouldn't make a lot of sense.

He had a face that looked lived in. Because it was.

As this flight progressed, Paul recalled the first time he had been in an airplane. At age eighteen, on 6 January 1967, after taking his step forward for the Albany, New York Local Board #27, he was bussed with eleven others to the airport for a flight to Columbia, South Carolina—Fort Jackson. It was suspected that one of the tricks the Army used in those days, to keep desertions down, was to send the draftees to forts far away from their homes. Enlistees from the Northeast, on the other hand, were sent to nearby Fort Dix, New Jersey, where weekend passes were a possibility. Of course, the fact is, the enlistees still had to endure another year or two of Army life for that small privilege. And even worse, they earned the contempt of the draftees as they shouted out their serial number in the mess lines, their prefixes being RA for Regular Army. A draftee's prefix was US, as in United States, but the owners of this prefix insisted it stood for Unvoluntary Servitude. Proper grammar was not as important as an expedient acronym.

As bad as the draftees headed for Columbia felt, it could have been much worse. Twenty-four men took the step forward that day. You didn't have to swear the oath of allegiance to America unless you wanted to. However, when they called your name, you had to take the symbolic step forward—or go to jail. After calling the names, and taking the step, they administered the oath. Most of the guys mumbled it anyway. Then came the big shocker. A young Army sergeant announced, "Last names beginning with the letter A up to the letter Mc, advance to the rear three steps. Welcome to the United States Army. You men remaining in front, welcome to the United States Marine Corps."

Wow. You could have heard a pin drop. Those poor bastards. Most people didn't know that the Marine Corps was drafting people during the Viet Nam War. Some of those people were standing in the front rank. One guy said to the sergeant, "Sir, I can't go into the Marines, I'll never make it." The uniform's reply surprised everyone in its kindness. "Son, if you can get one of those Army people standing behind you to take your place, and you take his, I'll be happy to do the required paperwork." The unfortunate turned and looked at the new soldiers, but they averted their eyes. He turned around and hung his head. To this day, Paul wondered what happened to that poor drafted Marine.

Paul, the new Private, vomited in the propeller-driven airplane, as did three of his new travel mates. Not one of them had ever been on a plane before. With false bravado, they pretended that the lightning and rain outside the windows at 17,000 feet in the air didn't cause the nausea. It was because they all went out drinking the night before the journey. And it was true in at least one case.

The oldest draftee, a married former high school football star, was placed in charge back in Albany and did a great job of getting everybody to switch planes correctly at Atlanta. By the time they arrived in Columbia, the men were all old hands at flying. And scared to death.

The confusion of the Army's Reception Center was highlighted by the new language that these new soldiers were going to have to learn. It had little to do with nomenclatures and a lot to do with keeping a straight face as the orders and directives were screamed at them. "All you mens what don't have no coat will get an extra blanket, of which you will sign a hand slip for it, and it would behoove you mens which have got the extra blanket to keep it close to your shivering asses as you will be court-martialed and sent to the stockade if you mens lose the extra blanket that my army has given you out of pity for your sorry asses." Paul was happy he had a coat.

After ten days of uniform issue, shots, buzz-shave haircuts, tests, speeches, forms, work details, not much sleep, and one draftee going bonkers and getting taken to the shrink, the men were herded, in real cattle cars, to Basic Training.

The ten weeks of Basic went fast, and Paul learned a lot. For one, he learned that there was always one guy worse off than everyone else in at least one skill.

Unfortunately, that guy was the same person a lot of the time. But Paul was quite happy that he wasn't often that person. Sometimes, he wondered how some of these guys were going to survive the Army, much less Viet Nam.

He was also quite adept at imitating one of the ornerier corporals, and his dead-on impression, unknown by Paul, was overheard by the senior Drill Instructor one night. Those guys were everywhere and heard everything. However, the D.I. liked the impression so much, he had him repeat it for the other cadre of NCO's as Paul was doing his K.P. duty. This made the other D.I.'s and his own leader stay off Paul's back for the most part. Plus, the fact that Paul, who had never fired a rifle in his life, scored expert on the rifle range. This was also a big deal for the boss men as they usually had side bets with each other as to which platoon would shoot the highest scores. Paul figured that the reason he shot so well was that he didn't have to "unlearn" anything, like the good old boys from the south. He listened to exactly what the range fire instructors said during training and applied the requisite skills. Although he liked firing a rifle, he didn't like cleaning one, as it was never good enough to be accepted by the armorer.

He learned to wait until the armorer wanted to go home, and then he accepted all the rifles, with just a cursory look. Paul was a quick study.

Paul was proud when he graduated Basic, having been promoted to the next pay grade, as only ten soldiers out of two-hundred and thirty received this distinction. He was notified as to where he would be sent to school and what his Army job would be. Paul was to stay right at Fort Jackson, no leave, for the next ten weeks to learn to be a radioman. He was okay with this because, in 1967, everyone figured the war would be over in no time, and ten weeks was forever.

When he got to radio school, he was told that the top ten percent of graduates would be sent to Fort Gordon, GA for radioteletype school eight more weeks. He graduated first place in radio school. Eight more weeks, no leave. *How long could that war last,* he thought?

The sixty days at Fort Gordon went by quickly, and there was no end in sight for the war. Two life-changing things happened down there at radio teletype school—RTT—that were significant for Paul.

First, he met Bobby Ray Jackson, a good ole boy from Gaffney, a town near Spartanburg, SC, who, along with Paul, was made a Squad Leader during the duration of the school.

Paul couldn't have been more different than Bobby Ray. It was amazing that these two human beings got along at all and, in fact, were fast friends. The southern soldiers were, for the most part, enlistees as opposed to draftees, verifying the suspect rule of sending the enlistees to forts close to their homes. But it seemed to Paul these guys were gracious in taking to their homes the northern draftees with weekend passes, who hadn't been home in a long time. And their families and friends were also kind to them. The New York boys called these guys "grits." And of course, they called the northerners "Yankees." Nothing real original there.

Bobby Ray was short, compact, opinionated, highly racially prejudiced, asthmatic—which he lied about to enlist—and a good soldier. He and Paul got hooked up initially when it seemed like every other word out of Bobby Ray's mouth was "nigger." After a few days of this, Paul said, "Hey buddy, I don't like that word." The retort was, "I ain't your buddy, and I don't give a flyin' fuck what your sorry Yankee ass likes and don't like."

It was on.

Paul went after Bobby Ray's neck with his hands. Bobby Ray was more surprised than scared, and it took him a moment to get his balance, at which point he got Paul in a pretty good headlock. Paul rammed him into a tent post, and the general-purpose tent—GP medium—collapsed on the two of them. They both started laughing, and the brawl was over. Still laughing as they righted the tent, neither the fight nor the reason for it was ever brought up again. Bobby Ray just tried hard to avoid saying "nigger" around Paul, and Paul pretended he didn't hear it when Bobby Ray slipped. Bobby Ray could never understand why a white guy, like Paul, would be offended by that word. *Friggen Yankees, nuttier than a squirrel's balls.*

Bobby Ray and Paul were inseparable after that day. They just watched their verbal boundaries and joked about common enemies, the Army, the brass, good pussy, bad pussy, lifers, and Jody. Jody was the fictional guy, a draft dodger, who stayed home and got your girlfriend, your car, and everything else of value that you left at home—as in the marching or running chant, "Ain't no use in looking back. Jody's got your Cadillac." Your girlfriend was known as "Little Mary Rottencrotch" or some other lovely moniker.

Truth be known, very few of these guys had girlfriends, let alone Cadillacs. Most of these guys had nothing, maybe a mother and father who loved them and said they were proud of them, even though they were worried to death about what would become of them.

The overwhelming profiles of enlisted soldiers in 1967 were poor southern white kids, poor northern white kids, black kids far more than their demographic portion, and many, many Hispanic kids. There were draftees from places that weren't even States, like Puerto Rico, The Virgin Islands, and Guam. Some of these kids didn't speak English. You didn't have to articulate anything but your trigger finger, as far as Uncle Sam was concerned. One of the favorite excuses for joining the Army was that "The Judge gave me a choice, Army or jail." This took the onus off the guy for enlisting, whether it was true or not. And in 99% of these cases, it was not. Paul's favorite was when one of the soldiers, known as "Fast Eddie," stated, "I signed up for Tahiti." The recruiter told this guy that he could put in for Tahiti. You could see why they called this guy Fast Eddie.

Second, Paul signed up for Jump School.

One day, the platoon was brought to the theatre to hear a pitch for Airborne volunteers. Bobby Ray had already been guaranteed jump school after radio school by his recruiter, but all were forced to listen to the pitch. A tall, good looking Hispanic sergeant, with master jump wings on his chest and soft cap gave the spiel. Paul thought that this was the most impressive looking soldier he had ever seen.

Jump school was three weeks long, four weeks if you considered "zero week." It would commence directly after graduation from RTT school. Four more weeks in the States. Again, *how long could that war last?* Paul signed up immediately. He and Bobby Ray and a religious guy with the unlikely name of Posie were the only airborne volunteers from his tent. Even though the other guys said they were crazy, you could see that they really respected them for signing up as their eyes were always wide when they were talking to them, kind of like puppies waiting for a command. Posie, a conscientious objector, who would not carry a firearm into battle, and Paul were the only draftees from the platoon to do so.

Paul and Posie graduated from RTT school and were promoted to Private First Class, Pay Grade E-3. This was important for a couple of draftees. Bobby Ray didn't fare as well, remaining an E-1. He was supposed to automatically make Pay Grade E-2 in four months but got into an altercation with a young black soldier, and both were held back from promotion. It really wasn't even Bobby Ray's fault. Paul was at the scene and saw what happened. The seventeen-year-old black kid, from Mississippi, was in line with the rest of the platoon, waiting to sign out on a day pass to go down to Augusta, GA. The problem was that he had on his dress army green slacks and low quarter shoes along with a civilian tee shirt and straw cap. You could either wear your dress greens or your civvies but not combine them in any way. Bobby Ray, honestly, and not in the least bit maliciously, told the young trooper the rule. He knew the CQ—Charge of Quarters—signing out passes would not let him go out dressed like that. The black kid told Bobby Ray to "mind his redneck business." It was on, once more.

It didn't keep Bobby Ray from graduating radio teletype school though. Posie, Bobby Ray, and Paul were sent to the travel center barracks, where they met up with about forty other guys who volunteered for jump school. They were placed on an Army cattle car bus and transported to Fort Benning, GA. for paratrooper school. Of the forty-three guys on the bus, an astonishing twenty-seven of them were draftees. Some wanted the extra $55 a month parachute pay, which was quite a supplement to a Private's $92.30 monthly salary. Some, like Posie, figured, as a sky soldier, he could do the most good. Some, like Paul, thought this was an acceptable way to waste four more weeks in the States. *The war should certainly be over by then.* Some, like Bobby Ray, were trying to outdo their fathers. Some guys wanted to impress girlfriends back home wearing bloused boots. Some guys wanted to beat somebody up when they got home, possibly their recruiting Sergeant. And one guy had no idea why he was on this bus.

The weeks at the jump school were physically taxing. A lot of upper body work and tons of running. But at night, after 1800 hrs., you ate chow, cleaned your gear, shined your boots, wrote letters, and bullshitted with your buddies. The biggest surprise of jump school was how easy it was to jump from an airplane. You had to do five jumps to get your wings, and the biggest problem was not getting injured in a PLF—parachute landing fall—so that you would be medically set back and forced do it all over again. And your crotch was red sore because of the harness that pulled on your balls when the chute opened. Other than that, it was stepping out of a door in the windy solitude and serene views before doing it again. On graduation day, when the Generals were making speeches, telling the new troopers they were all going to Viet Nam, some of them would die, some would get wounded, and what an honor it was to serve, it started to dawn on Paul that this war wasn't ending just yet.

Then it was time to wait for orders. Orders came in the daily mail, and you could tell where you were going because of the APO—Army Post Office—number, fore-runner to the zip code. If you got APO 96-something, you were going to Viet Nam. Of the 130 guys who got orders on graduation day, 106 got APO San Francisco 96-something. The Nam. First, they had to go to the Republic of Viet Nam—RVN— village for four days. This was a little homemade village, complete with tunnels and booby traps and punji sticks that all the Nam-bound troops, even the cooks and clerks, had to go to. The training was run by returnees from Nam and truly scared the living shit out of the troops, especially the cooks and the clerks. After that, the poor unfortunates got thirty days leave. Bobby Ray and Posie got thirty days leave.

Of the remaining troops, sixteen were not eighteen years old yet or had a brother serving in the combat zone. Either way, it bought them some time. One guy got a direct appointment to West Point, a *friggen miracle* as he was a draftee. His armed forces entrance scores were so high, he was asked to take the SAT's, aced them, and was presented with the chance to attend the Academy. He used to work at a plumbing parts store in Indiana. Five guys got orders for Korea. And two guys got orders for West Germany. The Germany guys only got twelve days' leave. Paul got twelve days' leave. He was happy he didn't get thirty days' leave.

Bobby Ray asked Paul to go downtown that night to celebrate. "Yeah, sure," Paul said even though he was a little embarrassed by his own good fortune. Paul and Bobby Ray tried to convince Posie to go out with them, but they knew he wouldn't. "That's alright, you boys go out without me." He didn't drink or smoke or swear, but he wasn't stuck up about it, just didn't party. Paul figured if Posie got killed in the Nam, the Viet Cong who shot him would meet a pissed off St. Peter somewhere down the road. Bobby Ray was quiet around Posie like he just couldn't figure him out. He wasn't used to this modest brand of courage, and it scared him. Posie was the other person he didn't say "nigger" around as well.

There was a place in Columbus, GA called the Whiskey-A-Go-Go. It wasn't the world-famous Whiskey-A-Go-Go, but neither Paul nor Bobby Ray knew that. Paul felt sophisticated in this bar, where it was legal to drink at eighteen. The go-go girls in their fringed outfits and their fat, stretch-marked legs did their impressions of the frug, the jerk, and the pony. They all looked remarkably bored. Of course, they, along with two barmaids, were the only females in the whole place. It was crawling with drunk, whacked-out paratroopers, wannabes, and three of the biggest, meanest looking bouncers below the Mason-Dixon Line. It was a train wreck looking for a place to happen. For some reason, it seemed to Paul, southerners had to do this weird rebel yell thing whenever they came within thirty feet of alcohol. When Bobby Ray let out his first war-whoop, Paul knew it was going to be a night to remember.

Chapter 2

Save the Tomatoes for Packy

Back in the plane, Paul's mind flashed from memory to memory. He left the Whisky-A-Go-Go in Columbus, and his random-access memory took him to a cold, dark college bar in Albany, New York, in 1969, where it was easy to pick up a babe for the night. Paul never thought of hooking up as much of a challenge as he had a tremendous line of bullshit. And a job.

On this night, at twenty years of age, about three months after his discharge, and about 75% of his journey to full-blown alcoholism completed, Paul saw a dark-haired, tall girl in a mini skirt standing at the far end of the bar, alone. She was staring into her drink, tight-lipped. Paul walked over and said, "How ya doin?" She glared at him. Didn't smile, didn't frown, didn't do diddly. Strike one.

Paul said, "So, do you go to school?"

She fired back, with a bit of venom, "I'm a TEACHER!"

Strike two.

Paul said, "Oh, I'm a janitor. My name is Paul."

She smiled. "I'm Kathy."

Base hit.

They drank some beers and Paul told his usual lies. It was probably apparent that he was lying most of the time, but he was so goddamned good at it the fib receivers didn't generally care. His intelligence, humor, and potential always shone through—until he got "the click."

"The click" was when he got just enough booze in him to give himself over to feel that the world was okay. It came to him as a distinct switch in his brain every time. *There it is, I'm okay now.* Coasting.

But he wasn't okay.

Click City meant blackouts, outrageous behavior, pathetic fistfights, buckets of vomit, and the worst—next day remorse. The only way to get over the next day remorse was to get the click again, and this time it would be different. But it wasn't. Ever.

Kathy was quite impressed with Paul. For one thing, he was tall. Tall girls always want a guy to be at least within reasonable eye-level range. Another thing, he was funny. Not like her stuffed shirts, fellow tweed people who had tenure. They didn't have to survive and deal with the frustrations, anxieties, and horrors of warfare. Black humor and escapism were just a couple of the coping mechanisms employed. As were prayers, drugs, alcohol, sex, and cigarettes. Paul was a janitor for the phone company. When you started a career with the phone or power company, you had to start as a janitor or meter reader, just so they could see if you were an asshole or not before investing money in you to go to lineman's school or splicing school.

The bar closed at three in the morning, so they went to the diner on the corner and got omelets. Paul didn't eat his eggs, just a couple of charred home fries. He had a lot of trouble with the eating portion of life. Plus, he didn't want to fill his belly with food as it interfered with the uptake of the click juice.

Kathy told him, watching him ignore his omelet, "I'm from a little rural town outside Cattaraugus."

Paul thought, *how in the hell can somebody be from someplace outside of Cattaraugus? What could possibly BE outside of Cattaraugus? Maybe farms, cows, hermits?*

Anyway, he got her phone number. He didn't even try to score, though he was clearly on third base with a good lead. He was pretty much clicked out anyway, but he knew he was going to call her because he took his time in writing her number down. In big letters, he wrote "Kathy from Hooterville—met last night at Daddy's" so that he would remember the next day.

Kathy was twenty-five years old and taught high school English. Paul was twenty and mopped floors. They were perfect for each other, or so Paul thought. The pair went out on dates, and the dates usually went like this: Paul would show up, relatively buzzed. They would go to dinner or for a sandwich, which Paul always ordered but rarely ate. Movie. Bar. Kathy's place.

The best times for Paul were when he was buzzed, in bed, after the obligatory conjugal wrestling match, and low, slow-talking to each other. It was Kathy's best time too. The rest all felt like bullshit, but those precious minutes made life enjoyable again. Kathy was so smart and would use words like "egregious" and "appalled." Paul made her laugh with tales of his adventures. He tried but couldn't explain to her the gray world he had come from. How could Paul discuss something he wasn't even close to figuring out for himself? A lot of the time, she would parse, but never correct, his stories. She would tell him about symbolism and icons, and she made him realize what saving the tomatoes for Packy really represented.

Paul had three siblings. In the pure, white trash, Irish shanty lexicon, just about everyone's name had to have an Irish diminutive—or at least a semblance of one. Paul's name was safe, couldn't destroy that one, so they went with Paulie. The micks and the ginzoes had a real knack for making every name end with a "y" or "ie," no matter how old the guy they were talking about. His sisters were Kathleen—Kitty, Theresa—Tessie, and Patrick was Packy. For some reason, known only to God, Paul's aunts and his grandfather decided that Packy really loved tomatoes. They had a garden in their postage stamp backyard where they grew radishes, tomatoes, and squash. When they harvested their bounty, the standing rule was, "Save the tomatoes for Packy." Packy didn't love tomatoes. He also didn't dislike tomatoes. In fact, he was completely ambivalent about them. However, whenever anyone in the family got over to Troy to see the two spinster aunts and the grandfather with the colostomy bag, they got tomatoes. "These are for Packy, he loves 'em." And they were dutifully returned to Patrick. Sometimes he ate them. Sometimes they were included in the daily repast, with the rejoinder, "Packy was nice enough to share his tomatoes." As far as hunter/gatherers go, it was Packy's fifteen minutes of fame.

Kathy explained to Paul what this all meant.

"It made your aunts and grandfather feel an attachment to their relatives, on a personal level. It also helped them in their crop choices for the year. They couldn't leave Packy's tomatoes out of the harvest. So, they felt good."

Sure, it made Packy feel special. He couldn't very well tell them at this point that they were out of their minds, right? So, he always thanked them profusely for the goddamned tomatoes. Kathy explained, "It was the connection to Packy that was important, not the object." This made sense to Paul. He thought Kathy was the smartest person he had ever met.

Kathy had secrets. She occasionally cried, usually while reading. Paul thought she was really into that story. She never really explained what the bandage under her right shoulder was for. At first, Paul assumed it was razor burn or something, but as the weeks went on, he knew it was something else. So, one night, after the social duties were accomplished, he asked her. He couldn't really see her too well in the dark. And it was good that she was in his arms. She said, "Paulie, I have Hodgkin's Disease." Paul didn't know what that was, but it sure sounded ominous. She had never called him Paulie before. Being the self-absorbed prick that he was, naturally, the first thing he said was, "Oh, is it contagious?"

"No, it's cancer," she said.

"Ummm." Paul was desperately trying to think of the right thing to say. He knew this was a watershed moment in both of their lives.

"What do the doctors say?"

"Well," she sighed, "most of the treatments are experimental, but they're hopeful. Every day, new potential cures are found."

Paul thought, *Sure, just like back in '67, how long can this war last?* He really was at a loss now. Couldn't think of anything to say. He just held her close, all night. Taking her to see the movie version of *Love Story* last month was probably not in her best interest.

And now he knew that he loved her, and that confused and scared the bejesus out of him.

He moved in with her the next day.

Chapter 3

"Don't much care what that Yankee boy does."

Back in NY, the plane landed, and Paul squeezed down the aisle, stiff from the ride or his years—he couldn't decide which. As he ducked to exit down the portable stairway, he couldn't help but think about how Bobby Ray wouldn't have been able to make this trip—what with his artificial leg and missing arm. He wouldn't have put up with the kind flight attendants fussing around him, trying to make small talk, and professionally ignoring his body's remaining parts. Funny, this was a guy that Paul had jumped from airplanes with, and now he wouldn't even be able to ride as a passenger anymore without a big hassle.

Robert Raymond Jackson III was born in 1946 to a self-professed, self-trained, auto mechanic dad and a school lunch-server mom. He was the only child, which was a good thing for Bobby Ray as his parents couldn't really afford one child, much less children. It also stretched their tiny mobile home, albeit with a lovely skirt. His crib for the first nine months of his life was a dresser drawer in the kitchen, between the bathroom and the only bedroom. Bobby Ray never grew up feeling deprived as most of the kids in Cherokee County were in similar straits. The only thing he truly hated was to manhandle the kerosene cans into the house for the two months of the year when you needed heat at night. He didn't like the way the fuel made his clothes smell, but since most of the kids were in the same boat, the hazing at school was kept to a minimum.

He was good at three things: footballing, fist fighting, and car fixing. His dream was to make a living out of the first two, but inside he knew his fate was probably destined to be the latter. He was a fullback when being a fullback meant something. Short, compact, and ran straight forward. Bobby Ray only had one fumble in his whole high school career, a record that still stands. His nickname was the rather complicated, "make way for Bobby Ray," but it fit him perfectly.

Fistfights were usually after school affairs, well-announced, and ended after a couple of punches and some wrestling before the older guys would break it up. Rarely, he fought boys of color, but when he did, it usually didn't end so gracefully. No matter who got the best of it in these encounters, there was a lot of residual animosities, name-calling, and bitterness. You could sense that there was something different about these fights.

Bobby Ray's dad, Robert Raymond Jackson II, taught Bobby Ray about cars. He could fix almost any car, though he was partial to Fords and didn't like the Jap or Kraut cars. He could drop an engine, repair a trannie, or change a headlight. Didn't matter to him, he was always greasy during the daytime and at night if he had to help a neighbor get fixed up. But he was clean as a whistle for three things: going down to the VFW post to get a beer on Tuesdays and Friday nights, going to church with Mrs. Jackson on Sunday morning—a promise he made to himself during the war, the big one, and kept—and, of course, going to the Klan meetings.

The Klan was alive, active, and vibrant in South Carolina in the late '50s and early '60s. Pop started taking Bobby Ray to some of the picnics and later to the assemblies. Bobby Ray was about twelve years old then. As the high school years passed, Bobby Ray was enamored of the camaraderie and fellowship of the members. He was well-received, always complimented on his football prowess. "Here comes our Bobby Ray, the strongest man in town. Good to see you, Bobby," some of the Klanmen would announce when they saw him show up with his dad. It really wasn't political at all to him, just his way of life, like his dad's and friends' and neighbors'. He would proudly say, "This is Klan Country" to anyone who would listen.

Bobby Ray never had any difficulties with the black players on the team, though. There was a mutual respect, even though Bobby Ray thought that he had to work much harder to be good, and to most of the blacks, it seemed like came pretty much naturally. This didn't affect the mutual performance, and Gaffney HS went to the South Carolina finals, winning the championship two years running. Bobby Ray was voted MVP in his senior year.

His asthma was exercise-induced, and he had it all his life. It didn't really affect his fullback chores as he would just lower his helmet, legs under him, and run straight for three or four yards. Then get a rest. But when the colleges came to evaluate him, they noticed the deficiency during the long runs, workouts, and chest auscultations. That, coupled with his below-average academic talent, was not good news for Bobby Ray. The scouts and coaches told him, "Unfortunately, son, we can't offer you're a scholarship, what, with those grades, but you can try out as a walk-on." *They can kiss my ass,* he thought.

He helped his father work on cars, but there wasn't enough work for the two of them, so he took a job driving a forklift at a grocery warehouse. He earned a little more than minimum wage. Everybody in Gaffney did.

Bobby Ray wasn't too worried about the draft board as he figured his asthma would keep him out. Anyway, he had just turned nineteen and didn't have his "report for physical" letter yet.

He had a girlfriend, Mary. She was a natural blonde who wasn't book smart, but she was clean, polite, and a lot of fun. The pair got on well. Movies, necking in the car, speedway, and it wasn't too long before they were in the sack. Bobby Ray didn't use rubbers. "No feeling," he said, so he went bareback, always pulling out in time. Or so he thought. Soon, Mary was with child. She told Bobby Ray and her parents, and he told his dad. They all decided the forklift job was secure, and Bobby Ray and Mary should wed. And wed they did. Two months after the news. And seven months later Charlene was born at a robust twelve pounds. "Charlene, if you'da been a boy, you coulda been a fullback," was the first thing he said to his infant daughter.

Four months later, Mary was with child again, and Bobby Ray lied about his asthma and joined the Army to become a paratrooper. He didn't have hospitalization at the grocery warehouse and was still paying for Charlene, so he figured, the Army can pay for this one. Which they said they were happy to do.

"Just sign here, son. Don't worry, we'll keep you close to home if we can. After all, you're not a draftee, and who knows, that war could end any day. We have lots of forts in North and South Carolina and Georgia. No sweat."

After the traditional going away barbeque at the VFW, celebrating Bobby Ray's patriotic departure, Bobby Ray arrived at Fort Jackson, South Carolina.

So, the unlikely duo of Paul and Bobby Ray was born. Bobby Ray took Paul to his home on weekend passes sometimes. Paul enjoyed himself and ate the best peach pie he ever tasted in his life. Bobby Ray's mom started making peach pie every time she knew Paul was coming. It was a little like the tomatoes for Packy, without the symbolism, but Paul really loved the peach pie. No ambivalence up in here.

One night, after dinner, Bobby Ray told his mother and father that jump school was starting in a week. His mom said, "Can't you reconsider? After all, you have a wife and two children here who need you."

"But Ma, I signed up for this, and besides Paul is going with me."

She said, right in front of Paul, "I don't care what that Yankee boy does, you're my son!"

After that, the peach pie kind of lost its luster for Paul.

Two days after the fight at the Whiskey-A-Go-Go—not the real one—Bobby Ray and Paul said their goodbyes to each other. Posie and Bobby Ray got on the bus to RVN village, and all Paul saw of Bobby Ray after that day was an S rolled mattress on the barracks floor.

Until two years later.

Chapter 4

Cloudy Days and Billy Flynn

At the small Cattaraugus county airport, there were a total of two car rental agencies, or rather, stands. When the Hertz guy had to go to lunch or to grab a smoke, the Avis guy would pop over to his kiosk and cover for him, and vice versa. It was kind of the end of the line in the car rental career hierarchy. Hertz was open, so Paul rented the better of the two cars available. He could see the car from the window of the terminal and walked out in the lightly falling snow. It started right up, but took a while to heat up, and as soon as it did, Paul was on his way. He had several places to go to. He had to look at an old house, occupied by only one person now, look at the local high school, and go to Walmart's. First, he decided to stop at one of the local "watering holes" for a Diet Pepsi because the free water on the plane didn't cut it. He needed a real drink. Funny, even at this late stage of the game, he still wouldn't touch a drop of alcohol. It had been twenty-six years since his last drink, and he wanted to keep the streak going. Especially now.

The joint smelled like every small, local bar he'd ever been in, and his thoughts were running wild with crammed memories competing for his attention and rumination. He remembered, back in his twenties, many times of walking into a bar in downtown, the real downtown Albany at nine AM, needing a "healer." You didn't have to be embarrassed about this situation as everyone in the bar was in the same fix, except the owner. He saw old rummy-nosed Billy Flynn, retired from a locomotive plant, greeting him every time with, "Billy Flynn here, Errol's my brother, and not as good lookin'." And then everyone would laugh. The bartender/owner would smile and say, "Nazdrovia, Paul, what'll you have?" It wasn't really a question because he knew that Paul needed a shot of whiskey, double, in a tumbler type glass—because the hands were shaking—with a Hedrick's Beer chaser. If he had some dough, he'd say, "Ziggy, give 'em all one and don't forget yourself." More likely, though, he would just say thanks.

These bars don't change, nor the people in them.

The bars were the junkyards, Paul thought. That was where the wrecks of society stowed themselves. It's where regular folks came in sometimes to see if there was anything worth salvaging, or maybe there would be a serviceable human being with a few good miles left before their inevitable demise. As in the histories of most formerly proud wrecks, the inhabitants of the junkyard emanated days gone by and spoke lovingly of the wrecks gone forever. They, most of the time, kept a loud, witty discourse going. You couldn't sense the despair if you were in the middle of it. But, if you came in from the outside, or didn't speak *Wreckese*, you would feel the sorrow. And waste. The steady, unheard clock ticking away the seconds, minutes, hours, days, and in some cases, years of their miserable lives. Always to be replaced by a new, ravaged face, hiding a broken mind and spirit.

In those days, Paul used to get wasted in the morning, lasting 'till about six pm. Then he would drive, or stagger home and pass out, to be up by ten pm and do it again until about four am. Unless he had to go to work, which he was good about. He always had a hangover but would pop a couple of healers, do some Visine for the eyes, and eat about fifteen Luden's cough drops—which fooled absolutely no one. He always suffered at work, but he was convinced that a real alcoholic would do anything to keep a job. For two reasons,

One, he needed the money to drink, and

Two, most importantly, if he had a job, he couldn't possibly be an alcoholic, *right?*

The problem with the drinking for Paul was that he was fine until he got that "click." Then something went haywire. He would get loud and obnoxious. Most folks who knew Paul could recognize this stage coming and would leave before he could go after them. But, invariably, some stranger or lingerer would become the target of his wrath. Surprisingly, Paul didn't become banned or "barred" from many establishments because he was a steady customer, had a job, and always apologized, even when he didn't remember what he did, which was about 90% of the time.

But when Paul and Kathy lived together in her rented house, Paul was still somewhat in control of his drinking, and the incidents were kept to a minimum. Kathy didn't believe Paul had a drinking problem. "I think ... it's just a readjustment from the Army. A phase. You know, it was tough for him. For everybody. And he had a traumatic childhood that he never dealt with, Sylvia," he heard Kathy divulging over the phone one night. In addition to those two, she believed he had a self-esteem problem phase.

She never raised her voice, ever. Nor did he ever raise his voice to her. Never a reason to, for either of them. She tried so hard to make him happy, buying him clothes that were stylish since Paul's idea of style came directly from whatever Smokey Robinson, James Brown, or The Temptations were wearing. She had a Mustang, and so did he.

They were always happy when they were together, and the only time Paul felt like he could do without drinking on a given day, was when they *were* together. But she taught school during the day, and Paul was assigned as a janitor on the night shift, which gave him time to drink during the day and go out with the other janitors at night. During the week, they didn't see each other. On the weekends, Kathy was busy correcting papers, reading and crying softly to herself. Paul was usually asleep on Saturday. Sunday was their day together.

One evening, right after dinner—a half stick of broccoli for Paul, a chicken potpie for Kathy—the phone rang. The caller asked Kathy if Paul was there. She handed the phone to Paul, with a querulous shrug. "Hello" said Paul.

"You Yankee dog, what comes out of the sky?"

Paul responded, "Birdshit and paratroopers, where the hell are you?"

Bobby Ray said, "I'm in a hellhole in Conshohocken, Pennsylvania, near Valley Forge. Gotta be hundreds of amputees from RVN."

He said he'd been there for about seven months, getting fitted and training for his prosthetic leg and arm. Before that, Osaka, Japan after two weeks in a hospital in Chu Lai, RVN. They wanted to get him closer to South Carolina, to be near his family, but his wounds were so severe they figured the best course of therapy would be in Pennsylvania. Paul instantly had a sneaking suspicion that it was the Army's policy, in direct contradiction of the enlistee/draftee orientation location, to keep the small-town boys out of the sight of the locals since this would bring the war too close to home for some of its most ardent supporters. Wouldn't surprise him a bit.

During this conversation, Kathy noticed a tenderness and vulnerability in Paul's voice as he talked to Bobby Ray that she had never experienced before, even during their warm, close conversations in bed at night. It intrigued and scared her at the same time. *Who was this Bobby Ray guy? Why hadn't Paul ever mentioned him? Why do I have to grab just snatches of this man's life? What is going to happen now?* Kathy left the room, and the conversation went on for about fifteen minutes, a world record for Paul. They exchanged addresses and made tentative plans to meet up in PA. Paul was upbeat after the call, Kathy noticed. But he didn't really say much besides that it was an old Army buddy that called.

Bobby Ray did mention that he heard Dave Posie was killed in an ambush. He was in the same unit as Bobby Ray, but different companies. Bobby Ray said he liked Posie, a lot. As did Paul. And even though he didn't realize it until just now—a lot.

Kathy was getting sicker. She was always pale, being a mick, but lately, she was paler. She was tired and terrified but hid it well. A couple of times, she had to go into the hospital for two or three days at a stretch, but Paul was attentive to her needs. One time, there was a bad blizzard, thirty-five inches of snow, and Paul walked over twelve miles to get to the hospital to visit her. At that time, Paul met Kathy's parents. In Paul's head, it went well, but found out later, in a letter that Kathy had inadvertently left lying by the bedside, that her parents were hoping that she "could do a little better." Paul wasn't mad about it. In fact, he was impressed by their ability to see him for the loser that he was. But Kathy was furious, and the relationship with her parents became quite strained for a time.

One day, when Kathy was teaching, Paul went to his buddy's house to help him paint a bathroom. That took about an hour and off they went to a local eatery so that Paul could nibble at his food, watch his buddy eat, and drink some beers. Their waitress was a pretty girl named Irene. Paul did his usual flirting, and she was receptive. "Here's my number,"she said, pointing to the digits at the top of the check, and Paul called her the next day. He never said anything about living with Kathy when they went out. When she asked where he lived, he shrugged and said, "In the area." Irene didn't inquire further, and maybe she liked that Paul was so secretive. That night, the two just drank, laughed, and eventually, on the third date, she invited Paul to spend the night at her basement apartment. He went. Stayed for three days.

He never went back to living with Kathy.

Sometimes he stayed with Irene, or his buddy, or slept in his car. He was losing it. Kathy was heartbroken. She was teaching when he got his stuff out of her house. He felt like a prick, and he didn't know why he was doing it—he just did it. Kathy was the one person he loved. He didn't love Irene or Betty or Rita or Mary or any of the women and girls he had taken advantage of during the sixties mores.

He suspected that he was frightened by this love.

Or any love.

He was correct.

It was a cloudy day when he pulled his stuff out of Kathy's. It reminded him of Germany. Germany was overcast most of the time. The Brits got badmouthed for having gloomy weather, but Paul thought the Germans got more clouds. It just seemed to suit Germany.

When Kathy came home that night, she looked in the bedroom closet last, knowing what she would—or rather wouldn't—find. It was bare on one side. There were a couple of sport coats, slacks, and dress shirts still hanging. Paul didn't take the clothes she had bought him. He just couldn't. She sat on the bed and cried.

It started raining hard. But it was crystal clear in Germany.

Chapter 5

The Minnow

In frigid NY, Paul decided to have another Diet Pepsi as he sat in this strangely familiar barroom. *Why am I drinking Diet Pepsi? I'm certainly not real concerned with weight gain at this point.* Glancing around at the clientele, for the first time seriously, he saw a guy, three stools down, who had no nose. No nose, just a hole. Nothing covering it. *What the fuck?* Did he lose it in the war, car accident, cancer? *Jeez, cover that baby up!* The guy was quite animated, talking away to the bartender, just like he had a nose. He had the remnants of a ham and cheese sandwich in front of him. Could he taste it? Could he smell things as it was loaded up with spicy mustard? *Why are all these bars friggen Fellini movies?*

Staring into his Diet Pepsi, Paul remembered 1970. After his six-month stint as a janitor for the phone company, Paul was sent to lineman's school. Or "the pole yard" as it was known. This was a surprise to the other janitors, one of whom was a phone company bigwigs' son, because they all had been there longer and were waiting to get picked for the school. Paul was surprised as well, but his work record was by far the most impressive. He always showed up early, never turned down overtime, smelled a lot like cough drops, and worked like a dog mopping floors and emptying waste baskets. Paul decided that the phone company was a fair and just employer.

Line school was three weeks long, just like jump school. First week, classroom, theory of telephone pole stuff—as in, the power company oversees the top half of the pole and the telephone company has the bottom—and some of the lineman terms. Second week, climbing the poles, at which Paul, inexplicably, excelled. Third week was driving and operating the trucks, known as polecats. They were big, with tiny cable trailers, and top heavy because of the augur in front. This was a cinch for Paul because in Germany he had to drive five-ton trucks, with ammo trailers attached, through the forest and had to back them up between giant pine trees and camouflage them. He had his share of dents and mishaps over there, so driving class at the pole yard was child's play for him. Sober or drunk, no problem. You needed a class one chauffer's license to drive a polecat, and the guy from New York DMV came to the pole yard to give the written and road tests. Paul was first to drive, passing with excellence. Out of the other seven guys, only two passed. The failures had to do another week of driving, but Paul got assigned to a five-man line gang.

The foreman's name was Black Pete, which was peculiar as he was a white guy with blond hair. And a robust appetite for anything containing ethanol. They were assigned to do "recon" work, which, unlike the Army's use of the term, stood for reconstruction. Every day, they were out in the rural areas, taking down so-called "idiot wire." This was twelve pairs of telephone cable that were strung from poles only twelve feet off the ground. Black Pete's crew had to take the wire down and pull the poles from the ground. Then the "digger," a small rototiller contraption, would dig a three-foot trench between where the poles had been to make a bed for the underground cable replacement wire. It was easy work and fun in the summer and fall. Spring sucked because of the mud, and winter was a nightmare. But Black Pete was a resourceful and cooperative boss. He knew every bar and liquor store in upstate New York, so finding booze was not a problem, nor was the partaking of the said spirits. These guys, usually only four because it seemed like somebody always had a day off for some reason, worked like dogs for the first four hours of the day, then two would nap in the truck and two would work/drink.

Paul thought he died and went to heaven. Always receiving terrific progress reports, everybody said he was a cinch for splicing school and then foreman. He was on the phone company fast track.

Then came the strike. Communication Workers of America—CWA—went out, nationwide. And nationwide, it lasted four months. Then they went back.

All except NY, another three months.

Then they went back, all except the Capital District, another four months.

Paul was out of a job for almost a year. CWA gave him $20 a week because he was single, married guys getting $40. That stopped when the union went back after the first four months.

Paul picked up odd jobs, including, at one point, driving a molasses truck because he had a class-one chauffer's license. Problem was, he didn't have a clue as to how to drive a partially full molasses truck coming down a mountain, and at a hairpin turn on Route 9 in Vermont, he tipped the tractor-trailer over, molasses pouring all over the road. That site smelled like pancakes for the next three years. The Vermont troopers weren't too happy with Paul. They locked him up for two days and released him with the caveat, "Stay on the New York side of the border." The National Molasses Company quickly relieved themselves of his driving services.

He started driving a taxi, nights. What an education he received in that vocation! He found out where the all-night bars were. The whorehouses. The card games. He met some good guys. Hustlers, but good guys. He had one buddy named Welch Green, a real dark-skinned black guy and a cab driver, except, he leased his cab, so he could do what he wanted. And the last thing Welch Green wanted was passengers. He was a pimp. And a good one. The man had class. He had the best hats, coats, and shoes, and man, he could talk. The ladies loved him.

Paul and Welch became tight. He started running some of Welch's ladies—his overstock, so to speak. Welch took Paul to his favorite all-night bar, known as "The Rabbits," where you literally had to check your weapons at the door, off-duty cops included. They walked in the door, and of course, everybody knew Welch, approaching him with an, "Aye, Welch, my man!"

"Whatcha see is Whatcha get," the hit by the Dramatics, was on the juke. Two tables were filled with players with a waitress, assigned specifically to those tables, in the back of the room for the fast ghetto card game of Tonk. A couple of people dancing. Everybody in the joint was high and mellow. Paul was down *widdit.*

Since he was attached to Welch, Paul was accepted by all and always had a pretty lady on his arm. He was becoming well-known in the rotation. The hookers would spend a couple of weeks in Albany, then move to Hudson, then move to Elmira and then to Buffalo and so on. They would be fresh faces to the johns during these rotations. Welch oversaw the Albany Division. Despite all the stereotypes of pimps, Welch was never seen to raise his voice or arm to a girl. He was respected, but he would kill you if he thought he was being played. Nobody played Welch.

"Paul, man, maybe you should slow it down with the booze," Welch tried to tell him. "It's getting a little out of hand, don't you think?" Since Paul was leasing a taxi, he didn't pick up fares either and could drink while he worked to his heart's content. And his heart was always content. Paul continued his downward spiral, despite Welch's warnings. To say he wasn't aware of the problem would be wrong. He just figured it would end okay someday. "Nah, I'm doing fine. I promise," he said to Welch.

One afternoon, on the way to the taxi garage, Paul stopped to get a healer. He sometimes would try to force down a pickled egg from behind the bar because he knew that you had to eat something, sometime. He went in to take a dump. It been about two years since he had taken a firm shit, but this one felt solid, so he had to look. There, outlined in porcelain, was a tiny turd, which looked like a minnow. Paul was proud of the minnow at first because it wasn't a bloody, sticky mess like usual. But then he thought, *That's the best I can do. A tiny, little turd, from a big man like me? That's my life in that bowl, a little hunk of shit.* He was shaken and hurried to get his taxi.

Paul thought about that minnow all night long, as he drove from girl to john, to bars to pick up his regulars, and back to johns to girls. As he got drunker in the natural course of his evening events, he laughed at the turd, but he vowed to himself to eat a little more food and at least get the size of the fish in the bowl to be legal.

Chapter 6

Bloods

Still staring at his diet soda at the local tavern in Cattaraugus, he stayed with his recollections. Maybe it was the nose guy or the memory of his voiding production that reminded him about Bobby Ray's problem. Or, more correctly, just one from his cornucopia of problems. Bobby Ray had to wear a piss bag for a while as he was catheterized for over a year. The embarrassment of changing the tube had long since faded, but the pain was real enough. Bobby Ray thought the male medics or nurses were a lot better at changing it than the females. Probably had some sympathy for him.

Bobby Ray had arrived in the Republic of Viet Nam in August of '67. There were half a million U.S. troops there at that time. Westy asked, and Westy received. For every "front line" trooper, there were about seven rear echelon troops. Front line trooper meaning infantry, artillery, or the small armor units. Cooks, clerks, supply guys, mechanics, radio operators, linemen, truck drivers—even bus drivers—base medics, chaplaincy guys, etcetera, had things a lot better in Viet Nam. The war was comfortable for some guys. Despite the letters sent back home, most of these guys had "three hots and a cot," and never heard a shot fired in anger. Maybe caught a mortar or rocket, but no big deal for the most part.

Not so for Bobby Ray. Bobby Ray's MOS—Military Occupational Specialty—was 05C2P. Broken down, 05—commo, C—radioteletype, 2—PFC, P—paratrooper. In the 506th Infantry of the 101st Airborne Division, Airmobile, this meant one thing. You humped the boonies with a radio on your back. That graduation in the top of your 05B class back at Fort Jackson was nice and all, but there was no need for teletype operators in this part of the Nam. Therefore, Bobby Ray humped his twenty-two-pound radio called a Prick 25. Well-named. It was said the first one to get shot at was the commander because it would cause confusion. Second to get shot would be the radio operator because he could call for artillery or airstrikes.

The reason he was second on the list was twofold. First, he was almost always standing near the commander, therefore pointing the leader out, and secondly, he was easy to hit because even if he ducked at the first shot, the bad guys just had to aim at the base of the whip antenna, where Bobby Ray was located. After a while, some of the radio guys got smart and used dummy antennas raised from the elephant grass, drawing fire and then firing back after the muzzle flashes gave the Viet Cong—VC, or North Vietnamese Army—NVA, positions away. American ingenuity at its best.

Camp Eagle was near a place called Phu Bai in the I Corps area known as the Central Highlands. I Corps was about evenly divided between the US Army and Marines, with an occasional Army of the Republic of Viet Nam—ARVN—unit thrown in. Literally. Contact occurred daily.

Artillery from scattered firebases spewed their lethal loads around the clock. The 105mm howitzer guys worked like automatons, stripped to the waist, business-like. They had to pay attention to the grid coordinates because there were always friendly troops out there patrolling or lying in ambush. It was the artillery guys' biggest fear to hit their own. It happened … more often than it should have.

Bobby Ray was usually one of the guys out there. The average patrol, search, and destroy lasted around four to seven days unless something happened to bring them back early. And, occasionally, forced them to hunker down for a few more days when extraction was impossible. When the patrol came back, after a brief back and after-action review, the boys usually got about four days to a week off to clean their weapons and then their asses, in that order. And to chill, drink beer, fight amongst themselves, sleep, write letters, jerk off, or better yet, go down to Phu Bai village and get a woman—usually just a girl—for bargain prices.

In the rear, there were two types of music, and therefore, two separate cliques. Country-western and soul. The lifers avoided these cliques and stayed by themselves. The CW guys were all wannabe rednecks, white, and drank beer and whiskey when they could get it. The soul guys were all blacks, Hispanics, and most of the northern white guys, and their drug of choice was marijuana. Beer was popular too. Some did heroin, but most didn't. The two clans avoided each other and talked bad shit regarding the other group. Fights were rare, usually when one of the groups strayed drunkenly too far into harm's way. No biggie. Bobby Ray was a CW guy.

This enmity did not translate to the field. Unlike the "In the rear with the beer motherfuckers," these grunts were a smooth, well-oiled machine in the bush. Both groups needed each other, and they knew it. Paradoxically, some guys felt safer out there.

It reminded Bobby Ray of his football days. Strange society, strange mores, blending, and adapting to survive another day outside of the wire. Only here, the squad sergeant was the coach, the lieutenant was the quarterback, and the grunts were the linemen.

It was, ironically, two black soldiers who carried Bobby Ray out of harm's way on that awful day. All the black soldiers called themselves bloods. They sure lived up to the name on that day.

It was a hot, humid day. Third day in the bush. The platoon had seen signs of the enemy—been shot at a couple of times—but no real contact. It was getting to be time to find a defensible place to put down for the night, send out a couple of listening posts, and maybe set up an ambush on the nearby trail. Bobby Ray was humping his radio and carrying a shotgun, a useful weapon when loaded with shot for the scrub brush on all sides. He never saw it coming. BALAAM! White light and lights out, Bobby Ray. Hit so hard and fast that he didn't even feel any pain. It was a rocket-propelled grenade—RPG—that hit the tree next to him.

While Bobby Ray was unconscious, a hell of a fight broke out. It was an L-shaped ambush, complete with claymore mines protecting the avenues of escape. Bobby Ray was the first to go down, along with his radio—one of two the platoon had, fortunately. Curtis Lee Mayo, a drafted former drummer for a soul group from Texas, and Conrad Dwyer, from Syracuse, New York, a drafted diesel mechanic trainee got to him first. Both bloods grabbed a piece of Bobby Ray's load-bearing equipment harness and dragged him into a ditch that was, thank God, not mined. Mayo put a tourniquet on what was left of Bobby Ray's right leg and then applied his "drive on" rag—a triangular bandage that was used as a bandana by most, another on his right arm, near the shoulder. Bobby Ray's face was ashen white, tattooed forever with the cordite and debris of the weapon. They gave him their only dose of morphine, even though he was out cold and screamed for a medic, but both medics were already dead.

Of the twenty-three-man platoon that was hit, only four troopers remained unscathed. Dwyer was killed in a mad rush at the ambush, and Mayo lost his right hand when the fragmentation grenade he was throwing had a "short fuse" and blew the hand off. Best guess today, he could only drum for the Beau Brummel's or Def Leopard. Both bloods were put in for and received Silver Stars. As did Bobby Ray, not so much for his heroism as for his wounds. It was a standard, unspoken practice, especially among the elite units, along with the purple hearts. These were appreciated because if you got three hearts, you were automatically out of the Nam. No rear or base camp. Out, home, land of the round doorknobs. Trouble was, you had to shed blood in combat operations to get a heart, so it was not a real safe method of getting the ride home on the freedom bird.

The rest of the battalion came to the aid of the trapped and decimated platoon's position. Two companies by ground flank attack. One by helicopter insert, which also extracted the wounded and, finally, the dead. Bobby Ray woke up woozy with stinging pains on his remaining leg. The hot shells of the M-60 machine gun firing from the chopper were ejecting directly onto Bobby Ray.

"Hey, motherfucker, cover my ass up, will ya?"

The bespectacled eighteen-year-old door gunner gave him a sheepish grin. "Sorry man, gooks all over the place!"

Bobby Ray passed out again.

Two of the four guys not hit were the platoon leader and his other radioman. So much for the first shot theory.

Dust-off landed at a Navy hospital unit at Chu Lai. There were so many casualties that day from all over I Corps that guys were taken wherever there was room, regardless of branch of service. Bobby Ray was triaged red, urgent, and quickly wheeled into a surgery room. It was covered in blood. Redneck's blood, lifer's blood, and blood's blood.

The docs didn't even try to save what was left of his right leg. It was just a femur hanging loose, held together by stringy muscle tissue. The right arm was so broken up with comminutions that, maybe, in a trauma surgery unit somewhere in the States, some function could be salvaged, but not here. No time. Not the right skills, not the right equipment. They sawed it off near the acromioclavicular joint.

At least he still had his nose—intact but peppered.

His wife got a telegram, delivered by taxi to her trailer.

We regret to inform you that SP4 Robert Raymond Jackson III, C/2/506, RA 11 256 456, was wounded in action near Phu Bai, the Republic of Viet Nam on 3 Mar 1968. He is a patient in USN Field Hospital at Chu Lai, RVN. His injuries are considered critical and life-threatening. We will keep you up to date on SP4 Jackson's condition as warranted. Please contact US Army, MEDDAC, Fort Sam Houston, San Antonio, Texas for further information.

There was no telephone number for Fort Sam Houston included.

You could say that, despite his horrible wounds, Bobby Ray survived. But you would, of course, not be telling the whole story.

Chapter 7

"I am sorry about your problems."

Back in cold Cattaraugus, leaving the tavern that starred the noseless customer, Paul momentarily forgot what car he was driving, but it came back quickly when he realized every other vehicle in sight was a pick-up truck of some sort. He thought about some of the cold days back when he was a lineman in New York in his early twenties. It had been a while since he'd thought about that job. *What the hell was going on here?* Life flashback. Introspection? Reflection? Purgatory? Apropos.

Almost forty years ago, Paul finally got the phone call he thought he was waiting for. "Come on back, strikes over. Report to the Watt. St. Garage tomorrow morning at 7:30." Paul was going to be a lineman once again. A little different this time though, as they had broken all the five-man teams into two-man teams. Black Pete was in the hospital dying of cirrhosis. His hair, now white, his belly distended, and his skin a bright orange.

Paul also had two hookers on the circuit staying at his small apartment downtown. One was a pretty good cook, and the other one had her thirteen-month-old girl with her. Paul kind of liked the company, and Welch appreciated Paul's largesse.

Welch was secretly happy that Paul was going back to his "real" job. The booze seemed to be taking a hefty toll on him, and Welch figured the regular hours and outdoor stuff would straighten Paul up. Paul thought so too, only this time things were a little different. For one thing, he didn't have the security of living with Kathy as a ground base and governor. And for another, he kind of liked "life in the fast lane." And *John Barleycorn* had a tight grip on Paul's ass by this time.

It was snowing like hell on the day he reported for duty at the line garage, and he was ordered, along with half of the other lineman and splicers, to go one hundred miles downstate to Poughkeepsie, NY, where the snow and ice had things in a state of disaster. The guys were happy, after all the time on strike, to walk right into some serious overtime. They convoyed down there, Paul wrestling with the polecat, where the front-end weight wasn't much help in the snow. But they made it to their motel.

The foreman told them they would be working fourteen hours on, ten off, every day until the region had telephone service restored for most of the area. They were fed at the motel and had brown bag lunches and dinners prepared for them on the way out the door.

Everyday.

No days off.

You could call anyone you wanted, free of charge, at the motel if the phones in the motel area were up, and the guys made sure they were up right away. This was the telephone company, after all. Paul had nobody to call.

They were paired with power company guys and worked well together, considering the hot stick guys had a superior attitude over the bottom half of the pole guys. Kind of like paratroopers over the rest of the Army, except now Paul was bottom half.

If he was worried about missing his booze, it wasn't for long. Alcohol was plentiful and constant, and the foreman didn't care. Morale was good. The guys showed up and repaired the wires. So Paul was back in heaven, except he assumed heaven wasn't quite this cold or windy.

They worked in Poughkeepsie for twenty-two days and nights. Fourteen on and ten off. Big bucks. Ordered back up to the Capital region, the boys came back like conquering heroes. Most had lost a little weight, were windburned, and were exhausted. When they pulled into the pole yard, they drove the trucks around to the back, where the mechanics awaited them, disembarked their rigs, and headed for the office. The boss greeted all with a "job well done" speech and directed them into the inner sanctum where the secretaries made sure that their payroll sheets and maintenance logs were in order. No one wanted to go out for a beer. Everyone wanted to go home. Even Paul, who didn't have a home. Just a small apartment with two hookers and a child in it. At least, they were there when he left.

When he got home, the place was empty. A note from one of the girls, Vanessa—if that was her real name—thanking Paul for his generosity. No balloons, no Welcome Home sign, just a note. He hoped someone would be there to welcome him. *Oh well*, a nice bath, soaking hot—no showers for this cold-assed lineman. Then down to Fitzpatrick's Pub to see his buddies. He went back to some semblance of regularity and tried to stay out of the taxi bars and all-nighters. Paul was trying to live a "normal" life again. As normal as it could be at 80 proof. And rising.

He missed Kathy. Maybe it was because he was back on the line, or maybe because he wasn't learning new, salacious habits. But he missed her, loved her, and wanted to call her. But he did not call. How could he? After what he did? He went to Fitz's and got plastered drunk, drove home, puked in his car, and fell asleep, left side of his face coated with vomit. The cold woke him up an hour later. He was stiff, sore, and drunk. The sixer he brought home with him was frozen solid. His vomit was also frozen. Struggling to get up the stairs to his abode, he collapsed on the bed, coat, clothes, barf, and boots still on, and slept. He pissed himself.

The boss gave all the out of town guys three days off with pay, so for Paul, it was four because he was on the polecat alert team nights on the schedule. So, Paul decided to go see about Kathy. He didn't call her. He just drove up to her rented house in the suburbs to see if her car was there. It was. Sitting outside for a while, he kind of hoped she would see his newly dented Mustang and come out. She didn't, and after a half-hour, he rang the bell. One of Kathy's friends from college answered the door, Sylvia, a pretty blond from another rural New York community, also a teacher. She had recently moved in with Kathy.

"Paul, what brings you here?" she hissed

"Kathy home?"

Sylvia backed up, not inviting Paul in, and silently motioned for Kathy.

When Kathy saw Paul at the door, her smile was warm and radiated joy. He got a lump in his throat. She charged him, ran to him, hugged and kissed him so much that Paul was now shedding tears.

He came inside, Kathy holding his hand. Sylvia sat on a lazy boy, reading a magazine, upside down, and tapping her foot rapidly. She was signaling for him to leave. Kathy didn't seem to notice, and Paul didn't give a fuck.

They decided to go down to Daddy's. Sort of a reminder of the night they met. Paul was hoping to literally sort of start all over, and Kathy was just happy that Paul was back.

They ordered beers and, for once, Kathy seemed to keep right up with Paul. This surprised him, but he didn't say anything. She seemed looser, sort of. Like she didn't care too much about anything. But it was so good to hold her close and even better to talk to her and listen to her. She was so *friggen smart*. Paul missed that, a lot. He didn't tell her much about the hookers, taxi, gambling, or drinking and just got vague when she asked what he had been doing. She didn't seem to mind, never appearing judgmental. He was back, that's all that mattered. They drank quite a bit.

"I want to see your apartment," Kathy announced, so they drove the three blocks quickly. It was small, relatively tidy, considering. Sheets that he had pissed on through his clothes were removed without her catching on. Bedroom stunk, though. Stale beer, vomit, and urine. Paul couldn't smell it. Kathy did but said nothing. She was laughing and pulled him down on the bed. They made ridiculously fast love, and then came the good part.

Lying there, looking in her eyes and talking about everything and nothing at the same time. Heavenly post-coital chit-chat.

She was sick, and weak, but hid it well. Paul saw the hole under her arm getting bigger, and the radiation burn scars were hard to miss. He asked, "So how's the Hodgkin's thing going?" She looked him directly in the eye and said, "I'll be lucky to live two more years." To which Paul replied, "Me too. Actually, I'd be happy with two." But he didn't mean it. She did.

So, they slept on the sheetless bed, covered by an Afghan rug-type quilt thing. Paul got up to pee and looked hard at the beautiful, vibrant young woman in his crib, wearing just these polka dot panties. This was always the first memory he had of her when he thought of her. And that made him mad, but that was the way it was. She was sleeping but smiling. Having never stopped smiling since she had seen Paul. Paul, for the first time ever, felt that his love was finally and truly requited.

His car wouldn't start in the morning, so he called in sick. School was closed for snow that day, so Kathy was alright. They decided to sleep in and pretend everything was just ducky. And this worked for a few hours until Kathy said, "Paul, I need to go home and take my meds, I can't miss a dose." He got a battery jump from the guy downstairs and drove to her house. Sylvia was waiting. Pissed. "Do you know you are two hours late for your meds? Do you have any idea how worried I was about you in this snow?" Kathy said she was sorry, and Paul just kind of buried his face, like kids do when they are scolded. Kathy rushed to the kitchen and got her meds. Paul could not believe how many medications she was taking. It was starting to hit home. She was absolutely sick!

Paul hung around for about an hour. While she drank tea, he had beer. She looked tired, so he kissed her on the top of her hair and left. He got into his car, it started right up, and drove to the end of the street. Pulling into a freshly-plowed lumber store parking lot, he cried, and then cried some more. He couldn't stop, smashing his fists into his steering wheel. It wasn't cathartic. It was primal. It wasn't cleansing. It was a supplication, a howl from hell. The hell he had put himself and her through, and the hell that they were both heading for.

He thought about getting some help with the booze and dreams. There was a Vet center downtown, a walk-in type deal. It was down by the Palace Theater. He drove towards the center. The snow was piled up in places, but the driving wasn't bad. Paul, of course, had driven through much worse in Germany. He liked driving in the snow. Everything was quiet, and it was kind of cool to slide around if you knew you had control. He got to the Vet center, but no parking in sight. Impulsively, he drove to the first bar he saw that had a parking lot. He'd try the Vet center tomorrow maybe. Baby steps.

He got drunk, drove home, and passed out. Called in sick again the next day and the day after that too. Then he took another week off, stayed drunk, and didn't even bother calling in at all. He just didn't give a shit. Just wanted to feel that "click" in his head that said everything was okay. The world was good. It'll all work out.

After being missing from work for three weeks, he figured he'd better see if he still had a job. Unsurprisingly, he didn't. He walked into the garage, went to his locker, and saw the note stapled to the door.

Mr. Fogarty, please report to Mr. Falkowski before starting work.

He walked into the boss's office and said, "I'm sorry, sir, I've got some problems." To which the boss replied, "I'm sorry about your problems. Your final check will be given to you when you return your equipment."

That was that. Paul wasn't a lineman anymore.

Chapter 8

The Assumption

Back to the snowy drive in Cattaraugus County. Traveling in slippery conditions was a little challenging, causing Paul to remain vigilant. Little drifts here and there were enough to stop him from using the cruise control. Wipers froze up a couple of times.

David Michael Posie came to his mind. Funny because he never really thought about that soldier from his past often. He wasn't good friends with Posie. Paul recalled that the conscientious objector CO paratrooper didn't initiate many conversations, but he was always willing to talk or to listen to others. He was usually to be found cleaning his rifle, shining his brass, or reading the bible. Most folks thought that all CO.'s were either in alternative civilian service or were medics. A CO paratrooper was a true dichotomy.

Posie's selective service classification was 1-A-O. This meant that he was a draft-ready person who happened to be a CO. 1-O's did alternative civilian service, and most 1-A-O's who got drafted went to medic school at Fort Sam Houston in San Antonio, Texas. There, they only did six weeks of basic training instead of the usual eight. This was because they didn't have to do the rifle range. From there, they went on to medic school. Most of those guys were Quakers. But Private Posie was a Seventh Day Adventist, and their rules were a little more flexible. They could carry and train on weapons if they morally felt justified. Not necessarily in a "just" war, but in an immediate just cause, as in protecting their brothers-in-arms. This was the paradox for Posie. When he got drafted, he specifically asked not to be given any special treatment. He knew there was a strong possibility the army would send him to the medics, but he decided to put the matter in God's hands. He would have gone to the infantry, artillery, or whatever. Having blind faith in that decision, he was assigned to radio school. And like Bobby Ray and Paul, he came out in the top ten percent of the class. Not to outshine his daddy, nor to delay his trip to the war, but because he always put 100% effort in all matters. This was also the reason he volunteered for jump school. He shot expert on the range.

Posie came from Escanaba, Michigan. Cold, dreary winters. His dad was a mortician, and Posie thought nothing of the corpses lying in the downstairs "living" room. He wasn't always a religious type guy. Ran cross-country and track in High School. Went to the junior and senior proms. Had a couple of girlfriends. He got to third base several times but never scored. Accepted at Michigan State University, he was an excellent student, which in 1965 was important as a lot of guys looking for college draft deferments. He took a liberal arts program but was not challenged, maintaining a 3.3 CI without, uncharacteristically, trying hard. On his way to the school library, he found a scuffed up Seventh Day Adventist pamphlet on the ground. He read the thing more out of curiosity than interest. What did impress him was the twenty-eight fundamental beliefs of SDAs, specifically, number twenty-two.

Christian Behavior. Posie was a detail/schedule-oriented kind of guy, and he liked the pattern and template of the sect. The Escanaba Seventh Day Adventist center was having an unlock revelation seminar one evening when Posie was visiting home. He went to the meeting, and he was hooked. Turned his life around and put that life in the hands of Jesus. In November '66, he dropped out of school, draft registration was changed from II-S—student—to 1-A-O. He was drafted on 6 January 1967.

All Paul really remembered about him was his dignity, morality, and diligence. He came out on top in basic training, radio school, radio teletype school, and jump school. Paul remembered shaking hands good-bye with him at the time he and Bobby Ray went off to RVN village before their thirty-day leave. Posie gave Paul a scapular of the Sacred Heart of Jesus to wear around his neck.

Paul thought to himself, *I knew he was going to die.*

Posie was assigned to Co. A, 2/506 Airborne Infantry. He saw Bobby Ray occasionally, but they were usually out in the field at different times. Bobby Ray was in Co C. The chaplain got to know Posie well, even offering him a job as chaplain's assistant. Normally it was a cake job, but this chaplain was a warrior. Posie was intrigued but felt his duties as a radio operator precluded this. He was experienced at calling in air strikes and arty and always had good commo, so he felt he owed it to his guys to do the job he was trained for.

He got to see the chaplain in action one night, though. At about 0200 hours, the mortars started coming in to base camp. A lot of them. Posie, reflexively, jumped from his cot, grabbing his steel pot and rifle, and hit the shelter trench just outside of the tent. As soon as he parked his ass in the trench, a shell landed dead on top of the next tent over. Kabluuee! Nothing left but some remnants of cots, equipment, and the pallets used as flooring. Outgoing fire suppressed the incoming, and all was quiet. Posie was the first into the former living space. Major Callahan, the chaplain, was right behind him. "Medic! Medic!" The cries went out.

One trooper was completely disemboweled. He was fruitlessly trying to stuff his guts back into where they came from. The more he pushed, the more spilled out. He kept repeating, "Mom, mom! Help me, Mom!" Another was lying on the ground on his side, looking like he was taking a nap. Not a noticeable mark on him. The medics loaded the guy with the guts out first, taking him to Sick Bay. They walked right past another soldier who had no legs, and his face was pretty much gone. He wasn't moving, so they assumed he was dead. They loaded the man who was on his side, napping, and finally, almost as an afterthought, someone grabbed his carotid pulse. There was none. He was gone, and he had that surprise party look on his face. The Major put his stole on, went over, and made a sign of the cross on his forehead. He got some oil and ashes from a little camouflage bag he carried.

It was just these three victims, and now they were in no big hurry as the guy with no legs and no face wasn't going anywhere. After about fifteen minutes, the medics came in with two body bags. They zipped the napper up and carried him to Graves Registration, which was the same place as Sick Bay, but when you were dead it was called Graves Registration. It was a good half hour before they came back for the kid with no legs or face. They started by putting what was left of his legs in the bag first, then grabbed him by the shirt and pants. The soldier with no face or legs rasped. He was alive and had been all along. There was no hyoid bone intact, so he couldn't speak, just make a hoarse rattle. His sight was gone as well as his hearing. The terribly disfigured patient sensed the others all around him. *Why aren't they helping me?* he thought.

They all assumed he was dead. Triage wasn't by the book, but it was understandable—to a certain point. He *friggen* looked dead. Posie was mortified. *The assumption.* Posie knew he would carry that weight forever. Major Callahan took out his bag of totems and tried to find a place on the head to anoint him. The priest-turned-warrior couldn't find a landing spot for his forefinger on the wounded man's head. So, he anointed his remaining arm. The sky pilot was crying, softly, to himself, and the guys pretended they didn't notice. They started carrying the patient to sick bay. By the time they got there, it had transformed into graves registration for this patient.

Posie died three weeks later, in the daytime, during an ambush. It was well set up, and after the first shot, everyone hit the deck and rolled to the side of the trail and started firing. Except for Posie because he never even heard the first shot. It deposited itself into his right eye.

The lieutenant tried to call in an artillery strike but screwed it up, so the enemy just hit and ran. They took off into the jungle, no more casualties. Eventually, a PFC got on the radio, gave the correct map coordinates, and everybody got out. Alive and dead. All of 'em.

It was a Holy Day. The Feast of the Assumption.

Chapter 9

The First Visit

Back in the New York tundra, Paul was messing around with the GPS device in the rental car but couldn't figure it out. He needed to find a Wal-Mart, and he wanted to check out a couple of addresses. One for a high school, the other a residence. He had the addresses—the detective agency had printed them out for Paul—as well as the location of the cemetery.

The Wal-Mart should be easy to find. He stopped at a gas station for a local map. Maybe he should have just asked the girl behind the register if she knew where these two addresses were, but even at this stage of the game, he wouldn't ask directions. Always the seeker, even now. Old habits die hard. He laid the map out in the front seat and found where he needed to go. First the school, then the residence. Little Valley HS, 25 Franklin Street, then on to West Street. He found a street sign and got himself oriented on the map. He headed toward the high school, full of anxious anticipation, as in the first time he visited Bobby Ray down at Valley Forge Army Hospital at Conshohocken, PA, back in 1969.

He remembered going into the ward building where Bobby Ray was located, following his directions to the letter. Paul brought along another buddy of his from Albany, a friend just out of the Navy to keep him company on the long trip down, and he supposed, to help break the tension. His buddy's name was Bernie, and Bernie whispered to Paul as they walked down the long rows of beds filled with amputees of all types, "Man, I feel like a freak cause I got all my parts." Paul didn't appreciate the humor—if indeed that's what it was.

Bobby Ray's loud southern accent found them before they got to his bed.

"Goddamn yankee bitch, looks like you brought another damned yankee here with you." Paul was surprised to see the formerly muscular patient's bones outlined. How thin Bobby Ray had become. He was sitting in his wheelchair—electric because he only had one arm. "They tried to give me a manual, but I kept going around in circles," Bobby Ray announced. Paul and Bernie laughed. Initially, they were overwhelmed in this Kafkaesque setting. Then Paul just sat down on the bed, as did Bernie, and put his arm around Bobby Ray's shoulder. "Welcome home, brother." Bobby Ray just looked at the floor and sort of sighed. "Yeah, Paul, a lot of guys didn't make it. I was really lucky." Bernie thought to himself, *he sure doesn't look lucky.*

Bobby Ray said that he could go off post until midnight and there was a bar right outside the main gate. "Let's go then!" replied Paul. Bobby Ray easily slipped off his blue caduceus laden army issue pajama top and then asked Paul to pull off his pj bottoms.

Bernie retrieved blue jeans and a cowboy shirt from Bobby Ray's locker and combed his hair. Bobby Ray put his prosthetic leg on and asked one of them to stand alongside for "balance." They were ready to go. It was a slow, torturous trip down the ward. Paul looked at these kids in their beds, *so friggen young.* One soldier with a missing leg was lying on his stomach, reading a superman comic book. Paul thought he looked all of twelve years old. Another guy with stumps for arms had the most perfectly coiffured Princeton haircut. *How in the hell did he do that?* thought Paul. Another guy was completely covered in gauze, missing a leg, with just a tube coming out of his nose. A trio of guys with a total of four legs and three arms were shooting craps in the corner. Paul thought he smelled reefer, but he couldn't be sure.

Bernie and Paul were happy to make it to the parking lot and out of Dante's hell. They got Bobby Ray fixed up in the front seat of Paul's Mustang. "Nice ride, man. The VA is going to give me a car allowance when I get the fuck out of here, and with a left footed gas pedal and a gear shifter on the left, I'm all set. Gonna get me a Road Runner."

They made it to the bar while it was still daylight. It was a neighborhood-type deal with the exception that the clientele was mostly male, young, recently wounded, and quiet. A few girlfriends and wives were also there. It seemed like the most of these women were trying to be cheerful and act like this was date night. They all had hollow eyes. The jukebox was playing "Okie from Muskogee" by Merle Haggard. They sat at a booth, ordered beers and smoked and joked for a half hour or so when a soldier entered the bar in army khakis and sat at the bar. He was about thirty-five years old and was the only G.I. in the place in uniform. He was a "BK." "BK's" were below-the-knee amputees, considered the best wound to get, the fabled "million-dollar wound."

"Aww, look the lifer got hurt. Did you step on a no-no, dodo? Or did you shoot yourself by accident? Or better yet, maybe your guys fragged your lifer ass!" Bobby Ray sneered. The soldier in uniform gritted his teeth a little but didn't take up the challenge. Paul and Bernie were surprised at this turn of events. They were taken aback for a few moments. Finally, Paul said, "Hey, Bobby Ray, lighten up man. Dude ain't bothering nobody." Bobby Ray muttered, "Fuck him, lifer bastard."

The target of Bobby Ray's venom got up, paid for his beer, and limped out. Bobby Ray yelled, "Yeah, that's right, lifer. Git the fuck out!" Then he sagged in his seat as if he couldn't catch his breath. Instantly, Paul remembered the asthma. "Where's your puffer, man?" Bobby Ray pointed to his left pants pocket. Paul didn't know how to work the inhaler, but Bobby Ray had enough presence of mind to take three big puffs. "Okay, I'm okay now." Bernie thought, *Friend, you're a long way from okay.*

When they got ready to leave, Paul and Bernie had to carry Bobby Ray to the car. He was lightweight. *Obviously,* thought Paul. *Like a kid.* He couldn't negotiate the prosthetic with the amount of alcohol he consumed. When they got in the car, Bobby Ray produced a joint and they smoked it in the parking lot, listening to the Guess Who singing "Undun."

"The grass helps with the asthma," Bobby Ray stated. Apparently, Bobby Ray was ahead of his time with the uses of medicinal marijuana. They carried him to bed in the ward. If anything, the place was even spookier at night, with the snoring, sighs and occasional nightmare shrieks. And Bobby Ray had been here for seven months and counting. They didn't try to undress him, just plopped him in bed. He rewarded them with a long fart.

Paul and Bernie headed for home that night. They didn't say anything in the car for a long time. It just seemed like they wanted to get as much distance between themselves and Valley Forge as possible, as quickly as possible.

Bobby Ray's wife and his parents were only able to come up twice in the seven months of Bobby Ray's hospital confinement. She brought the girls up once, but on the second trip said it was too much time on the bus for them. Bobby Ray's dad had lung cancer at this point, so his health wasn't up to the trip more than twice, and money was a real problem for his parents. They had to go on relief, never calling it *welfare.* Mary, Bobby Ray's wife, was getting along fine on her allotment check from the Army and her part time job at the laundry. But Bobby Ray didn't say much about any of that to Paul and Bernie. In fact, it seemed to the other guys that Bobby Ray didn't care too much about going back to Gaffney. They wouldn't have to "Make way for Bobby Ray" in his hometown for quite some time, it appeared.

As much as Bobby Ray bitched about the cold weather, he seemed to have a childish pleasure when it snowed, scooping his existing hand in the snow to make a snowball or telling Paul about all of the expletives he'd write if he could stand up to piss. He was comfortable with Bernie and Paul and liked their other friends. He didn't feel like the "freak" he thought he would become back in South Carolina. With his football glory days past, he felt he would be an object of pity. He needed time and space. New York afforded that.

Even though Kathy desperately wanted Paul to move back in with her, even offering to evict Sylvia, it was a no go. Paul took Bernie as a roomie, and they got along fine. Bernie was a head, and Paul was a drunk. Every now and then, one of them would take a foray into the other's vice. It was a social thing, kind of recognizing the legitimacy of your buddy's escape mechanism.

Bernie worked at a camera shop. He was pretty much a go-fer but would tell folks that he was a photographer, which, by God, he eventually became. And a damned good one too. Some years later, Bernie moved to Washington State and opened his first studio working out of his apartment. Paul thought Bernie was a genius because once he super-imposed a photo of a Budweiser pop-top beer can on Paul's forehead. Bernie worked his way up to make a good living with the photo shop and won many awards in that circle. He stayed away from certain subjects, like war, warriors, grief, and pain. Bernie found his niche in life. He was, unlike Bobby Ray, a lucky guy.

Paul drove his cab most nights, occasionally taking odd day jobs, like flower delivery, small tool repair and delivery, a stock clerk in a Radio Shack, feeding a gluey slurry into a machine that made plastic parts for refrigerators, and sweeping up a carpet weaving factory. These jobs couldn't touch the phone company for pay or benefits or any hope of a future, really. Shit jobs were aplenty during the late sixties and early seventies because all the guys who needed them got drafted. And the guys who didn't were milking their student deferments in colleges throughout the land.

But, mostly, Paul drove a taxi at night. It was instant money—you worked when you wanted, booze was a part of life, and you were sitting on your ass. The biggest fear was getting robbed, but all the bad guys knew that Yellow Cab

#22 was connected to Welch, so it was safe. Of course, some out of town junkie might not have gotten the message, but the odds were against it. Besides, Paul didn't pick up too many strangers, just the regular drunks, hookers, other cab drivers, and johns.

Bernie had a steady girlfriend while Paul tried to keep in touch with Kathy. She was always amenable, but ... she knew. Neither one of them ever said anything about the "future" of their relationship, but they both knew. Between the sicknesses of her cancer and his boozing, the only possible quotient was the terminal malignancy of the relationship. Plus, Paul had all the hookers he wanted for free. And he would occasionally pick up a civilian, just to see if he still had it. He did, but the crop was of a markedly lower grade.

Bernie and Paul would drive down to Pennsylvania on a Friday night, sign Bobby Ray out, and head for home. Bobby Ray was in pure heaven with these guys, especially Paul, who could usually get one of the girls to do her patriotic duty and tighten his scarred ass up, no charge. But Bobby Ray was not an easy lover. It wasn't his physical limitation. It was his mental state. He would be loud, drunk, obnoxious, and, ironically, prone to burst into song at the most inopportune times. Saying things like, "Bring that black ass over here and fuck me hard" or "Y'all just a ho and won't be nothin' but a ho' for the rest of yo' sorry assed life." Occasionally he'd smack a girl. When Paul got wind of it, he read the Riot Act to Bobby Ray, threatening to cut him off, figuratively. If Welch found out, he'd do it literally. Bobby Ray reset his limits to the Ethel Merman routine, and all was well in Sodom North.

But now, in the snows of Cattaraugus, Paul stopped remembering the past as soon as he saw the high school. Time to take care of business in the present. Even though it was all business, in his mind and spirit, from the past.

Chapter 10

"I'm not going to live my life here."

Paul saw the sign on the high school door that stated all visitors had to get a pass from the principal's office. He followed the signs and went to the second floor. The receptionist, a 40ish, attractive gal with glasses perched low on her nose greeted him. "Hi, would you like to sign in?" "Um, yes, I have an appointment with the principal, please," Paul stated.

She buzzed the principal's office, asked Paul his name, and two minutes later, Paul was sitting in the head office.

"Yes, Mr. Fogarty, how can we help you?"

Paul said, "I'm an author, writing a story on a particular girl from the class of '62. I have a letter of introduction and an appointment set up by the Albany Board of Education."

Paul's political contacts in the Capital City were many, due to his contributions to the Albany Democratic Committee. He continued, "I would like to use the library, look at some old yearbooks, and maybe take a walk—a lone tour of the school for background material. There wouldn't be any teachers still around from those days, would there?"

The principal replied, "Probably not, but there was one teacher at the school who graduated in the class of '62, I'm pretty sure. I'll double check it and get right back to you".

He gave Paul a paper sticky name tag which the receptionist had already written up, in beautiful cursive—Mr. Paul Fogarty. "The library is on the first floor. Please let us know if there's anything we can do to help." And that was that. Paul thought it was a good thing he wasn't a weirdo who preyed on high schoolers, and he was glad he was wearing a suit.

Funny, when Paul got down to the library, he didn't go immediately for the yearbooks. He looked for old books, forty-year-old books. He wanted to see if he could find the name Kathryn Shanahan written in the back of one. After a half hour search, he found one—*Poor No More* by Robert Ruark. There it was, in pencil, *K. Shanahan.* He could see, covered partially under the newly placed bar code register, a stamped date, *MAR 8, 1960.* Obviously not a floating inventory. Paul secreted the paper form, lightly glued to the back of the book with her fading penciled name and stuck it in his breast pocket. He thought he could feel Kathy's heartbeat coming from the pocket, and he got a lump in his throat. It was all coming together. She was dead thirteen years after checking this one out.

He went over to the yearbooks, starting with 1959, to see if he could find her picture in the underclassmen ménage. He didn't have too much trouble. There she was, in the "High Honors" group. With her braces and horn-rimmed glasses, she exuded happiness and confidence. This really affected Paul. He never thought of her as a little girl or teenager, always remembering the sick, beautiful raven-haired English teacher, as if she had been born into that role. Books '60 and '61, more of the same. High Honors, National Honor Society, Glee Club, Yearbook Staff. And then the '62 book, class valedictorian, a fact she never told Paul, as well as class president, editor of the yearbook, president of the National Honor Society, and on and on. Her yearbook quote was, "The woods are lovely, dark and deep."

A short, blond haired teacher came into the library and asked Paul if he was the one looking for background information on Kathryn Shanahan. Paul introduced himself.

"C'mon, Paul, let me buy you a cup of coffee in the teacher's lounge, we've got a lot to talk about." They left the library and walked the hallway together. "I'm John Gottstein, graduated from this high school in '62 with Kathy, and went on to SUNY Albany, where she also went before I transferred to SUNY Cobleskill."

He started right off with, "Kathy was the kind of girl everyone's parents wanted you to pal around with. She was always happy and always busy. I never saw her angry or too busy to stop and say hello. She wasn't just smart, she was brilliant. And I also remember her saying, quite frequently, in fact, 'I'm not going to live my life here.'" Paul asked about her dating life. John continued, "I remember her going to both the junior and senior proms with the same guy, Joey Urbanski. It wasn't like they were going steady or anything. I just think that they felt comfortable with each other. Joey was a wannabe jock, certainly not her intellectual equal, but they got along fine. Social security, if you will."

Paul had already learned from the detective agency that Kathy's last name when she died was Urbanski. This was the first time he realized that she married a hometown guy. Didn't make sense. But it would, later. Paul asked, "How about SUNY? Did you see much of her?"

John replied, "Kathy went to SUNY to learn. I went to party and dodge the draft board. We saw each other in the campus center, but we didn't have any classes together. She was pretty much into the books, no extracurricular stuff like here."

Paul said, "You know, she graduated in three years, Summa cum Laude, didn't you?" John answered, "Not surprised. Wouldn't have expected anything else."

"Do you mind if I ask you what this book you're writing is about?" John asked.

"Not at all, it's about an American hero who left us too early."

"Why Kathy? What made you pick her?"

"Bucket list assignment," said Paul quixotically. "Do you remember what kind of music she liked, by any chance?"

"Funny you should ask, she just loved Tom Jones. When I'd see her at SUNY, she always asked me, 'Have you heard the latest Tom Jones album, it's terrific!'"

Paul was so happy to have someone from her past that remembered her so well, but he honestly couldn't think of another question to ask.

"John, you've been a fountain of information, and I am in your debt."

"No problem, here's my card. Call me if you think of anything else. Oh, and I want a signed copy of your book!"

Paul laughed, "You got it, John. It would be my pleasure."

John finished his coffee and made a pistol finger gesture towards Paul as a good-bye. Paul shot back.

He was finished at the high school. Time for a cheeseburger. He couldn't believe that he was hungry, considering his terminal mission, but he was. Maybe it was the nose-less guy's cheeseburger that got him thinking about it. At least he knew he would be able to taste it. He went into a Friendly's restaurant and had a cheeseburger, fries, and a coffee. He took out the crib notes, written in the school, to cover his author story and looked at them. Tom Jones, *sheesh*. Then he reached into his breast pocket and found the signature card that she had signed so many years ago. His hand shook. He got a lump in his throat, set a twenty on the booth table, left, sat in his rental car, and cried.

Time for the next visit. Paul perused his map and found West Street. He wasn't too far away. This probably would be the hardest part of the wind-up, but he had a plan, and Paul usually stuck to his plans. *Maybe they won't be home,* he thought. He pulled up in front of a nice little bungalow-type house. The house was bought from the Sears catalog—no kidding, for real. In the early '50s, you just ordered the kit and built your house on a slab. It was great for the recently discharged veterans, contending with the housing crunch and money issues. Of course, over the years, additions were put on, and improvements were made. But the precursor to modern modular homes had held up remarkably well. Even more amazing considering the harsh winters in this part of the northeast. The house didn't have a driveway, but there was plenty of room to park on the street. The walkway to the front door was shoveled clean. Paul walked up and rang the doorbell.

The ornate chimes were out of proportion to the genus of the structure, but they worked. A small woman, dressed in sweater and slacks, and wearing eyeglasses, opened the door fully and said, "Hi, can I help you?"

Paul was amazed, even as old as this woman was, he could see Kathy's eyes. It freaked him out for a second, but he recovered long enough to say, "Hello, Mrs. Shanahan, I don't expect you'll remember me, but I was a friend of Kathy's, and I was wondering if I could talk to you about her for a few minutes."

"Oh, did you work with Kathryn or go to school with her?'

"Mrs. Shanahan, we've met before. In Albany Medical Center Hospital, in a raging blizzard, when Kathy was sick. I was her boyfriend at the time. My name is Paul Fogarty."

She looked down at the floor and said, "Oh yes, Paul, forgive me. I do remember you. Please come in."

She led Paul to a cozy living room and said, "I was just making tea, would you like some? Or coffee?"

"Tea would be nice, thank you," said Paul. She disappeared into the kitchen. In her absence, Paul looked around. He knew what he was looking for and found it on a bureau. Kathy's high school and college graduation photographs. He scanned them quickly, not wanting to get all weepy before Mrs. Shanahan returned. She entered with a tray of tea and cookies. Pouring for both, she said, "Mr.

Shanahan died in '84. They said it was a heart attack, but I know it was a broken heart." Paul knew exactly what she was talking about. "Well, Paul, what brings you here? What can I do for you?'

Paul was as direct as he could be at this point. "Mrs. Shanahan, when a guy gets into his later years, he reflects on his life. Mistakes, bad breaks, good ones too. And even though you can't live your life over again, I feel there are some fundamental things that have to be put to rest."

She looked perplexed. "I don't understand Paul, what are you trying to say?'

Paul just blurted it out. "Kathy was my true love. I just was too immature to know it. I think I broke her heart, and when I realized that she was the one true love of my life, it was too late."

She just stared before commenting, "Well, you know she married another fellow, Joe Urbanski, from right here in town."

Paul said, "Yes, I just discovered that a little while ago. Where is Joe now? Did he stay in town?"

"Oh yes," she said. "He's married again, a couple of years after Kathryn passed. Has two lovely boys. I believe one is in the service now." Paul didn't inquire as to whether he was still in town now as he had no intention of intruding on this man's life or memories.

"I'm going to tell you something, Paul. Don't know whether I should or not, but it feels right. Kathryn married Joe chiefly because she had no more medical insurance. The school district policy down there in Albany expired. She drained all her benefits. Her father and I told her to come home. We had savings and this house. She said, 'I'll be okay.'"

This was making some sense to Paul now. Mrs. Shanahan went on. "Kathryn did come home. Poor thing, she was so skinny and sick. She was here about a week when Joe called, and they went out. Next thing you know, they told us they were getting married. We were shocked, of course, but never let on."

Paul thought about the letter that the parents had written so long ago to Kathy regarding his own status in their eyes.

"And to be honest, Joe was very good to Kathryn, very caring. He is just a good man."

Paul said, "Yes, he sounds like a good man. I'm glad Kathy had someone to help her. I mean, of course, besides you and Mr. Shanahan."

She got a little misty when she said, "She didn't want to be a burden on me or her Dad. That was just Kathryn." Then she asked, "Paul, would you like to see some photos?"

"Yes, very much, Mrs. Shanahan. Very much, indeed."

She went into her bedroom and brought out three full albums and a small box.

"I'll just leave you alone with these while I run down to the store to get some milk, is that okay?" *She knows,* thought Paul, *she knows.*

Alone in the house, Paul delicately paged through the photos. Baby pics, summer camps, dance recitals, grade and high school buddies. Kathy was always smiling and happy.

Paul was starting to lose it again but held it in. In the box were medals and awards from school, girl scout pins, a Barbie doll dress, and a lock of beautiful brown hair. Paul held the lock in his hand, removed a small strand, and placed it in his breast pocket along with the signature card. He went into the bathroom, sat on the toilet cover, and cried. He heard the front door open, and he immediately got up, rinsed his face with cold water, and came out. Mrs. Shanahan didn't stare even though Paul was sure she heard him crying.

"I won't take up any more of your time, Mrs. Shanahan. I'll be going now. Thank you for your kindness, and thank you for Kathy."

He put on his overcoat, and she walked him to the door. "Where are you heading now, Paul?" She asked, even though she already knew the answer.

"I'll be going up to the cemetery, Mrs. Shanahan."

She looked at him with Kathy's eyes, placed her hand on his shoulder, and said, "Paul, Kathryn once told me, about a week before she passed, that she had no regrets. She said she knew love and love was eternal. She told me that she once knew a boy who showed her that. Paul, I think you were that boy, weren't you?"

Paul couldn't answer. He embraced her and left without looking back.

Chapter 11

Full, half or no choke?

Now it was off to Wal-Mart. He stopped at a Dunkin Donuts for coffee, and while in the shop, asked for a telephone book. He looked up the address, memorized it. In the car, he found the street the store was on and headed out. His mind was really flying now. The purpose of the journey was almost fulfilled. And, so far, without a hitch. He thought again about last minute details he may have overlooked but couldn't come up with anything. Things were starting to get a little surreal now. His concept of time was all messed up, his hands tingled, and he felt queasy in his gut. But he was calm, determined even. His sadness, this self-made cross bearing was going to be ending soon. Great mystery, the great darkness.

Paul truly believed in an afterlife. Not as God the bearded guy sitting on a cloud, but as ethereal energy that all humans and animals for that matter exuded. Energy cannot be created or destroyed, only changed in form. He would soon know all about the new form.

On his way to the superstore, Paul noticed a stream running alongside the roadway. It was more like a river, with the winter's snows washing down from the mountains. He stopped the car at an apparent rest stop—it was plowed, had a couple of weather-beaten picnic tables setting there. The rest rooms were locked, so Paul ambled off behind some trees to take a leak. *Coffee, tea, and old age are creeping up on me today,* thought Paul. There was no wind, and the late afternoon sun was pleasant. He found a large rock to sit and stare at the stream. The rock felt like a comfortable chair to Paul, affording a nice view, overlooking the stream and the pines beyond. It was a good place to think, perhaps to reconsider? *No way,* this was going exactly the way it was supposed to go. Penance is penance. Done deal. It's not supposed to be easy. As they used to say in the Army, "Hey, troop, if it was easy everybody'd be doin' it." Army had a saying for every situation. You just had to fit the theme into the scheme.

The stream made those refreshing gurgles and bubbling sounds that Paul thought were cleansing. He tried meditation once, with a cassette tape of gurgling, "babbling" brooks, but they included frog sounds and bird calls. Every time a frog *friggen* croaked though, Paul busted up laughing. Broke the mantra, so to speak. No frogs here though—too cold, so Paul wasn't tempted to deconcentrate.

It reminded Paul of sitting by a stream in West Germany, at Dachau, where he was stationed. That was a great place to be stationed, not only because it wasn't Viet Nam, but it was only twenty-two kilometers from Munich, where the nightlife was great for an eighteen-year-old draftee. His barracks, or Kaserne, as they were called, was an old SS training barracks and housed the concentration camps cadre since 1933. It was a four-story building, and each room housed two G.I.'s, but most guys had their own room because of the Viet Nam war manpower demands. The Kaserne had a PX, snack bar, movie theatre, motor pool, headquarters offices, quarters for Turkish troops, an enlisted man's club, an NCO club, Officer's club, and a large stockade, which is Army parlance for jail. The other half of the compound was the former concentration camp which housed a museum, the real crematorium, two rebuilt prisoner barracks, lots of footing framed rectangles where the old inmate barracks used to stand, and a road leading to the crematorium that was paved with the ashes of human beings killed and cremated here. Near the ovens stood a sort of convent type structure for Jewish nuns.

At night, they used to sing these dirges, which creeped Paul out when he was standing guard at the motor pool. He used to crawl into the hatch of a self-propelled eight-inch howitzer when they would start because it freaked him out. The camp was a great place to meet babes because they would come as tourists. Paul and his buddies could usually pick out the Americans and Brits and would just go right over and say, "Hey, I'm stationed here, want me to show you around?" Always worked. And if they got lucky, they would take them down to the hidden tunnels, under the camp and either lead them over to the club or just sit there and make out. No one ever thought about how creepy it was to pick up girls in a concentration camp atmosphere, at least not while they were stationed here.

One night while Paul was on guard duty, he thought, *I have eight months left here—maybe I should go to Viet Nam.* So many guys in West Germany had already been to the Nam, and so many guys were getting shipped over there from Germany—or, in army speak, "Levied." Paul reflected, *I am a paratrooper, only have eight months left, so I wouldn't have to do the full year-long tour.* He was also tired of the cold and being in the field on maneuvers sixty percent of the time. There was a good chance they wouldn't take him because he was a short-timer, and he could always tell his friends back home at least he volunteered. Army just ignored his request for transfer. Before he lost his resolve, he set off to the company clerk's office to put in his transfer chit. The piece of paper requesting transfer was called a 1049 form. You would write in longhand what you wanted, and the clerk would type it up and submit it to the proper channels. The clerk was a fat, lazy specialist 5th class who told Paul there was no sense in 1049ing to Nam because he didn't have enough time left to do the full tour. Was Paul willing to extend his induction status to go? This wasn't Army regulation but was the lazy clerk's way of trying to get out of typing the chit. Paul expected this, and said, "No, submit it anyway, D'Alessandro. You never know." So, the clerk snatched the paper, let out an exasperated sigh and said, "That will be all, Fogarty." Paul left the office feeling lighter. Another thing, sheesh, *how long could that damned war last?*

Back in present time, in cold country, a car pulled into the rest stop. An old couple slowly got out of the car, carrying a picnic basket. They looked at Paul perched on his rock and said, "Hello, nice view, huh?" He just smiled and looked out at the trees again. Paul thought, *they're old, but they're gonna outlive me.*

He fell back into his Dachau recollection. The shock came to Paul just two months after 1049ing. He was levied to Viet Nam. Apparently, the Tet Offensive of '68 took out so many guys that they were desperate, especially for radio operators. Paul almost shit himself when he got the news. But he coolly received the orders from the fat, lazy clerk, who seemed to be hiding a smile. Fogarty said, "No shit." D'Alessandro snorted, "be careful what you wish for." Paul parried, "This place sucks anyways." That was the best he could do. But his face was bright red, and he got a little dizzy. He half figured the lazy asshole didn't type up the chit and he was feeling more confident about the 1049 as he was down to six months remaining. Of course, there was good news and bad news. The good news was he would only have to do six months in the Nam. The bad news was he got no leave before going. He was to "clear" the Kaserne in two days, report to Rhein-Mein Airbase in Frankfurt, and arrive in Viet Nam, via army charter transport system by way of Oakland CA, Alaska, Hawaii just three days after leaving West Germany.

He was levied along with another soldier named Jack Palito, a draftee from California. Jack's brother had already been killed in the war. He didn't have to go, being a sole surviving son, but requested the transfer. Jack told Paul Germany was too fucking cold and "we are always sleeping in the snow and rain." Paul agreed but was tacitly thinking,

maybe the snow and rain wasn't such a bad thing. They
weren't in the field all of the time. Nobody was shooting at
you, and the biggest danger out there was wild boars that
roamed in packs all over the field sites of Grafenwoehr and
Vilsack. But if you fired at them, they usually took off. One
blood used to sleep on the roof of his truck because the boars
terrified him. And this guy had done two tours of the Nam.

Paul and Jack cleared post in one day and got drunk at the
Turkish soldier's canteen and smoked a lot of hash on the
second day. They went by train to Frankfurt and started on
the exhausting process of traveling to the other side of the
world. They became good buddies during this ordeal and
since Jack was a radio operator as well, they figured there was
a good chance they would stay together wherever they got
sent in country. Not to be. Paul didn't find out until years
later when he saw John Palito's name on the Viet Nam War
Memorial Wall in DC. He only lasted three weeks in
country. This made Paul burst out in tears, right there on the
mall, as if Jack had just been killed in front of him. And in
Paul's mind, for all these years, he was indeed still alive. Till
now. Those poor parents in California.

They landed at Bien Hoa airbase with about a hundred
and fifty other guys, and the first thing Paul sensed was the
unbelievable heat. And then the smells—diesel fuel, JP-8,
human shit, and body odors. Paul was nervous, as were the
other guys. The men that were quickly boarding the plane, in
khakis, seeing that the new meat had just vacated, were
merciless.

"You'll be sorry."

"Welcome to this motherfucker."

"Look at these assholes, won't make it."

And the most popular were the short-timer jokes. "Short-
timer," meaning the discharge date was days away.

"I'm so short I need a ladder to get into my boots."

"I'm so short I got to look up to see down." And "hours,
ladies, hours." But Paul and Jack were too curious and
nervous to get pissed, so they got on the bus and went to a

hangar and got their orientation briefing, which mostly consisted of, "If you fool around with the Vietnamese women, they have razors stuffed up their pussies. Cut your junk to pieces or can give you a form of the Black Syph whereas your dick gets so big you can throw it over your shoulder, and they send you to Guam for the rest of your life, 'cause there's no cure and you ain't allowed to bring that shit home." Kind of put the damper on anyone's plans for an exciting night out with a China doll.

They were issued a bedroll and were trucked to the transient billets just outside the gate of the Air Base, 90th Repo Depot at Long Binh. There, they were told to report every two hours to the company assembly area beginning at reveille and until retreat where they would receive their further orders. Jack got called at the first formation, off to a place called Ban Me Thout. He said goodbye to Paul, shouldered his bag, and was off. Paul thought that Jack, who was tall, looked like a kid heading for the chopper. Jack's face was beet red. Unfortunately, that was the memory of Jack that stood in Paul's head, forever.

Paul didn't get his call until late the next day. By now, there had been about a two-hundred percent turnover in the transient billets, so Paul was like the old veteran. The incoming soldiers treated him with respect. Crazy. Paul didn't even rate a helicopter ride. He got in the ass end of a three-quarter ton truck with his duffel and was driven a grand total of seven miles to his new base. Ap Thanh, assigned to the Headquarters and Headquarters Company of the 2nd Bn/ 503rd Airborne Infantry/173rd Airborne Brigade. The unit known as "the herd." It was a safe place, a *stay in the rear with the beer* place. Paul reported to the orderly room, which was a Quonset hut, told by the first shirt that he was in building number three, bed fourteen, with a wall and footlocker. Next morning, he was to draw his field gear and rifle. He met the radio chief, a sergeant first class lifer type who said, "You will work a regular shift on the radio

AN/GRC-46 in that van over there surrounded by the razor wire. You good with the '46?"

Paul nodded.

"Mess Hall is always open, there's beer after 1800. Don't smoke dope in the company area."

That was that. And except for a few stray mortar rounds, Paul had it easier than he ever had in West Germany. Everybody here had brand new jungle utilities, which they sure didn't need. You could spot the guys who had really been in the bush.

Their jungle boots were white with grime and sweat. And they wore CIBs—Combat Infantryman Badges. Not a lot of white boots but lots of CIBs on this post. So, Paul just skated for five months and even drew a twenty day drop on his flight call home. Paul was ashamed of himself inside. He knew people back home were worried and praying for him. How was he going to get wounded? Fall off a barstool? He volunteered for a couple of patrols around the perimeter, trying to kid himself that this was like combat. But when the kids were selling cokes out there, and the girls were offering themselves for a good time, he couldn't even bullshit *himself.*

Bobby Ray didn't get cokes on patrol. Bobby Ray got de-legged and de-armed on patrol. Jack didn't get pussy offers. Jack got his skull opened and brains leaking out into the mud on patrol.

Back at the rest stop, Paul saw that the sun was trying to set on the picnic area and figured he'd better get up to the Wal-Mart. Down by the stream, the old gent was skipping stones with his wife. Good peg for an old timer too. Paul wondered what they were talking about. Maybe they, too, lost a kid, in the war or to cancer. You never knew.

Paul revved up the car and made his way to the store. He went directly to the sporting goods where they had a fine display of fishing gear and rifles and shotguns. No pistols. Paul waited for the clerk, who was a young lady, already fructose portly, of about twenty.

He said, "I'd like to look at that Mossberg 16 gauge up there."

She retrieved the shotgun and said, "She's a real beauty and on sale this week. $239.99."

"Okay," Paul said. "Can I get some shells?"

She said, "Full, half or no choke?" to which Paul didn't have an answer.

"Umm, just give me slugs."

"Sure, just make sure you keep the choke off when you're using slugs, okay?"

Paul wasn't too sure of exactly what a choke was, but when she started unscrewing the tip of the barrel, he figured it out.

"Okay, fill out this form, and can I get you a cleaning kit?"

"Nah, just the gun and the slugs, thanks." He handed over three crisp new one hundred-dollar bills, took his bounty, and left. It was dark when he returned to his car. Paul didn't want to go up to the cemetery in the dark. He didn't plan it that way. It would be better to get a motel for the night.

The motel sign a few blocks from Wal-Mart flashed "VA ANCY," so Paul pulled in and got a room. Like all these motels, especially in the "off" season—as if there's an "on" season up here—the room was bone-chilling cold. You turned on the space heater full blast and eventually it got warm, then too warm, then cold, etc. Paul truly hated the cold. Reminded him of Germany, lineman work, but mostly of the long cold nights when his wacko mother would lock him out of the house all night. His dad was a fireman and worked twenty-four hours on and twenty-four off, and he had a second and even a third job. Dad couldn't protect him from this abuse, and truth be told, was likely glad to get away from the madness. She was a deranged woman, sadistic and pathological. Paul supposed having four kids by the time you were twenty years old would do that to a person. This would happen about three times a week when Paul was just entering his teen years. He would walk and walk. Finally, he would bed down in the project's storage rooms where the boiler was. Nothing worse than being wet, cold, hungry, unloved, and then pretend it didn't happen the next day. *It'll get better someday,* Paul used to think. But it never did. It just stayed the same. He didn't mind being locked out in the summer, kind of an adventure, though sometimes he was too tired to go anywhere. At least he never went hungry because he could rob milk bottles and the bread man. But the winter really sucked.

Paul hoped they had the History channel here. No luck. *Oh well.* They had A&E, *not too bad.* He watched a documentary on the flight of the monarch butterflies and thought about writing a letter or note but decided against it.

Stick to the plan, Paul.

Chapter 12

Make Way for Bobby Ray

Paul put the sleep timer on the TV so that he could doze after watching and listening to The Flight of the Monarch Butterfly. Thoughts bounced around in his head in the sort of half sleep daze he got into after taking one Ambien and two Benadryl tablets. He thought about the trip he had undertaken to Gaffney, South Carolina a few years ago. At that time, he hadn't seen or heard from Bobby Ray since the arrest, imprisonment, and release of his buddy.

Bobby Ray, having been discharged from the Army as a retiree—the benefits were better—decided to try to live up in New York State. He didn't want to go home to South Carolina. To Paul, he related, "They don't need another gimp to stare at down there." He called Mary about once a month almost always drunkenly and told her he'd come home soon. Though he asked about them, he never spoke to his daughters. Mary didn't understand why Bobby Ray didn't want to come home, but she was busy with the girls and the part time job. She went to church and prayed about these things. Occasionally Bobby Ray would tell her to get a divorce and find a guy with all his parts, but she didn't buy into that. Sometimes he'd call in a jealous, alcohol fueled rage and accuse her of fucking around. Deep down, this upset her, but she suspected he was drunk and just depressed. She'd respond to these tirades with, "Oh Bobby Ray, that's just the booze talkin' now."

He moved in with Paul and Bernie, and the destructive symbiosis for all three settled into place. Bobby Ray did buy a green Road Runner, with racing stripes and thrush mufflers, and drove like a maniac all over town. Whenever he got pulled over by the cops, they seemed to always feel sorry for him, and he never got arrested for DUI or anything like that. Sometimes they would take his keys and either drive him home or call a taxi. He could not drive at all in the snow and ice, but he sure tried. Once, he launched his car in a ski jump attempt over a snowbank. It landed on its roof after a complete 360. He then walked, with his artificial leg, the four miles back to the apartment, wearing just a shirt and pants. No coat or sneakers. It took him five and a half hours. He looked like he spent another tour in the Nam when he got home. Putting Staff Sergeant Barry Sadler's record album, "Letter from Viet Nam" on the hi-fi, he passed out on the floor. Paul took the unconscious man's wet clothes off. That's when he found the gun. Bobby Ray had a .45 Automatic pistol, Army issue, tucked in his waistband. Paul took the gun away, took the full magazine out, and the bullet that was already chambered and put the gun in his own bedroom. He'd talk to Bobby Ray about this when he woke up.

Turns out, Bobby Ray had a permit for the pistol. Permits in NYS were not easy to get, especially in Albany County. Bobby Ray presented his case before a sympathetic judge, also a war veteran, stating how he was an easy mark for muggers with his injuries. He also didn't have to prove how proficient he was with small arms, as his military record was tacit proof of that. "I don't hardly drink or do any of them drugs," he told the judge, and his lack of arrests for driving while impaired or other alcohol related things seemed to attest to that. So, Bobby Ray got his gun. Periodically, he'd pull the weapon out in bars but after waving it around a little, put it away. He got away with it until the night he put the gun to Steve's head.

Steve was the owner of a little neighborhood bar where Bobby Ray used to drink. He put up with a lot of crap from Bobby Ray, probably because he, too, had lost an arm in the big one, double-u-double-u-deuce. Bobby Ray took full advantage of Steve, borrowing money from him, drinking on the cuff, and, with his unpredictable antics, forcing a bunch of Steve's customers to other watering holes. He pulled stunts like unhooking bra straps, putting beer checks and toothpicks in other folk's drinks, stumbling around cackling like a goat. Once when a drunk, known for his great tenor voice, rose to sing after much cajoling from the den of losers, all eyes and ears were on the singer. Bobby Ray interrupted after the first verse and went to the jukebox and played James Brown's, "On the Good Foot." Bobby Ray's move, ironic as it was, did not merit that audience's approval.

One night, Steve said to his charge, "You're way too drunk to drive, I'll drive you home." Bobby Ray grunted his assent. Steve assisted Bobby Ray, intertwining their remaining arms, and when they got to Steve's station wagon, Bobby Ray pulled out his roscoe and stuck it in Steve's ear.

"Motherfucker, you just grabbed my dick! I knew you was a queer!"

Steve was mortified. He had never seen Bobby Ray so angry.

"I did not. Are you crazy? Get that thing out of my ear!"

Bobby Ray was unfettered. "I'm gonna kill you, faggot."

The noise had alerted a chronic lunger who was sitting by the window trying to breathe, and the emphysemic called five-o. Man with a gun. The first squad car was there in less than two minutes, sized up the situation, and called for back-up. "Man, with a gun, hostage situation."

This had two effects. First was the cop kneeling behind his open car door and pointing his weapon at Bobby Ray while yelling, "Freeze!" Second, in addition to bringing almost every cop in Albany to the scene, the news media, who monitored police and fire scanners continuously, mobilized. Bobby Ray was cornered, still having the gun in

Steve's ear, and said, "This faggot tried to grab me." By now, there were seven cops on the scene, all with guns pointing at Bobby Ray. A gigantic Sergeant said, "All right, son, lower your weapon and drop it on the ground. Kick it over here, and we'll get this sorted out." And Bobby Ray, smiling, complied. The cops rushed him, tackled him, and were a little stymied when they tried to handcuff him because his prosthetic arm had fallen off. So, they handcuffed him, on his remaining upper appendage, to a stair railing. Steve was shaken but asked the cops to forget it. Nope, the media was here now. Bobby Ray was unceremoniously tossed into the back of the paddy wagon and carted off to jail. He got a lawyer from the Viet Nam Veterans Against the War group who tried to get bail reduced at his arraignment, but no luck. He was charged with kidnapping, attempted murder, and a bunch of misdemeanors. Wisely, he agreed to a plea bargain. Three to ten years in prison for unlawful imprisonment and using a gun in the commission of a felony.

They sent Bobby Ray to Fishkill Prison, home for handicapped felons. His prison time was uneventful. Because of his army pension and war wounds, he was like royalty with both the correction officers and inmates. His fellow prisoners would pick up his commissary items for him so that he didn't have to travel down to the store building. His greens were always pressed and delivered to his cell. The guards would bring him contraband such as Playboy magazines and chewing tobacco. He had a plum job as a prison clerk and was quickly paroled after serving the minimum of two years and seven months. The board allowed him to finish his parole in South Carolina. New York was glad to be rid of Bobby Ray.

Paul and Bernie had visited Bobby Ray almost every month at the prison. It was good to talk to him while sober. When drinking, Bobby Ray was unpredictable in word and deed. Even though the sobriety was forced on him by prison, he was more articulate and thoughtful. He listened to you instead of just waiting to speak. Bobby Ray's father died soon after Bobby Ray was incarcerated, and he was denied permission to attend the funeral. Mary and the girls never visited. Mary divorced Bobby Ray after his first eighteen months was completed, and he got the news in a letter from his mother. She simply wrote, "Mary felt it was time to move on in her life. Her heart is broken, but she felt she must do what is right for the girls. She told me she will always love you, no matter what." He was okay with that. His army pension was attached, and child support was deducted before he got any money. He saved the rest of his money while in the joint so that he was flush when he got out. Paul had stored his Road Runner for him, so he had wheels. He could not drink, or use any drugs as a condition of parole, but there was a loophole in the latter. The stipulation allowed pain medication for his wounds. Bobby Ray took a lot of pain medication, although it wasn't for the type of wounds the authorities had known about.

When Bobby Ray went back to South Carolina, he moved in with his mother. She still lived in the same mobile home as before. Paul remembered the surprising warmth and hominess he first experienced many years ago when he came to this abode while on leave. Maybe because of the stark contrast to army living conditions, but even now, he felt a uterine kinship with this modest domicile. Bobby Ray had one of his old football buddies place a makeshift ramp with a railing so that he could get in the house more easily. Most days and nights, he was down at the local VFW, where he was a welcome patron at the bar. So much for the no drinking on parole stipulation. He would listen to Johnny Cash on the jukebox and pretty much keep to himself. Occasionally he belted out a tune.

He tried to reconnect with Mary, through the local grapevine, but she was seeing someone else now. A quiet, church-going guy named Terrance. Bobby Ray didn't take it personally, but he did telephone Mary about visitation. He saw his daughters when he could and took them for rides in his Road Runner. They were well behaved around him because their mother told them not to do anything to get Bobby Ray's anger up. Circumspection was the order of the kids' visiting days. After a while, Charlene loosened up a little, while her baby sister, Rona, remained vigilant. Charlene started talking about school, boys and maybe college someday. Bobby Ray tried hard to be a good listener and winged it with advice. He knew he wasn't a good example, but he tried hard to sound sage and proper.

It wasn't the Walton's, but it wasn't terribly bad either.

After a while, Bobby Ray met a thrice-divorced matron who worked at the post office where he would pick up his twice monthly paychecks and bills. She was friendly and always made a fuss when he came in. It was obvious they had an attraction. They became an item, and eventually, Bobby Ray left his mom's and moved in with Lu-Anna. He didn't abuse her, and she didn't cheat on him. It seemed an idyllic redneck relationship. She helped him with his medical problems, which were now not just war related, but alcohol related. Which was probably war related. His liver was shot, pancreas in a constant state of inflammation, lungs gone from smoking.

Bobby Ray died of cirrhosis on 6 Feb. 1996. He was anywhere between fifty and a thousand years old. He had a para-military type funeral, sparsely attended. Attendees included his long-suffering mother, Lu-Anna, Mary, Terrance, and the girls, along with the local VFW color guard. They shot their three-gun salute with blanks, only one of which fired, and played a tape of Taps on a boom box. It was a cloudy day, threatening to rain. After the service, the VFW had a buffet set up for the reception, and everyone went down there and told Bobby Ray stories, mostly about his football days.

His earthly existence gone, "Make way for Bobby Ray" became part of the local folklore, saying things like, "if it wasn't for that war, Bobby Ray woulda' been right up there with Larry Cszonka." Bobby Ray's prison stretch wasn't mentioned in the obituary, but his military and football heroics were. Charlene was the most visibly upset, crying, red in the face, choking back sobs, being consoled by Bobby Ray's mother. The VFW made Bobby Ray a lifetime member. Little late in the game for that, though. The VFW flag was at half-staff for the rest of the day. And even though the rain made the flag curl around the flagpole and stick to it like a wet rag, it was seemingly a fitting metaphor for a fallen warrior with feet of clay. Or at least a foot of clay.

Chapter 13

Mullets in 8mm

Paul's mind was squirming, recalling his trip down to South Carolina in 1998.

The bed in the cheap motel was comfortable, but understandably, Paul was having difficulty sleeping, despite the drugs. He played a game in his mind, the kind that usually helped him nod off. He recollected and played out different paths in his head, rather than the roads taken. Vicariously, he tried to project what would have happened in certain situations had he made different decisions. What if he hadn't pushed his alcoholism to the max? What if he took the appointment to West Point that the army had offered? What if he had never left Kathy? He was generally happy that the path chosen seemed to be the correct one. Except, of course, the actions and decisions in the case of Kathy.

He had been lucky concerning career and money-making. Despite his firing from the phone company, or, in this case, because of his firing from the phone company, he never had financial worries.

The booze had gotten to him badly in those days, and after a couple of dry outs at the VA, he realized that the problem wasn't going to go away by itself. He sought counseling, ironically, at the same outreach center that he disregarded during the snowstorm two years before. At that point, he was pretty much driving his cab full time, though he didn't really pick up too many passengers. Just worked his "huckle." A huckle was a cabbie's regular route consisting of picking up certain select passengers, running hookers, running booze, running johns, etc. It was probably close to impossible to give up alcohol while performing this huckle. At least it was for Paul.

The VA counselor asked Paul about the phone company job and the subsequent dismissal. It seemed to the counselor that the phone company was in violation of Paul's civil rights as a veteran. The VA man asked, "Paul, how did the firing happen?" When Paul recalled going to the pole yard garage and telling the supervisor that "he had some problems." The supervisor was supposed to hear Paul out and send his case to his superiors for a solution. That was the written phone company policy. The phone company supervisor sent Paul's case to his superiors, who simply rubber stamped his firing, no questions asked. The counselor told Paul that his problems were war related. At that time, PTSD was not fully recognized as a disease. Indeed, most Viet Nam vets were portrayed on television and movie screens as crazed, drug-addled maniacs. Most vets were just guys who tried their best to get the war behind them. But there were as many, if not more, mentally wounded than physically. Especially the *why him and not me* survivors. The counselor decided that Paul was one of these unfortunates. He said, "I'm sending you to a VA review board to see where your head was at, at that time. You may be suffering from a shell-shock type thing." In two months, the decision was medically certified, and the counselor finally told Paul the results of the board, handing over a business card for a well-known civil rights lawyer to see if he could get his job at the phone company back. Or at least a hearing from them. He was also allotted a VA pension of 60% disability retroactive to December 1968. It was a good chunk of change, but Paul never felt he deserved it.

Paul followed the advice, seeing no harm in trying, and bingo, he hit the litigation lottery. The phone company did not want to be a defendant in a case of possible veteran abuse, and Paul's attorney got a big—for those days—settlement out of court. Paul's share was $157,000. This was a huge sum of money in 1972. Plus, he got his VA check for $21,000 and monthly benefit. Paul was awaiting his final payout when another freakish event happened at about the same time.

One taxi company serviced the Albany airport. It was a monopoly, politically rigged, that had endured for years. An upstart taxi company sued the county for unfair trade practices, and a judge agreed. That decision meant that the airport was open game. The company that had the sweetheart contract, with salaried taxi drivers, who were mostly older, settled-down type guys, owned the same company that leased the taxis to Paul, Welch and about fifteen other drivers. This taxi company made a deal with the lease drivers to spend every day and night at the airport. They were called into the dispatch office and given the details. The manager, a tough little Italian guy named Rocco said, to all the leasees, looking clearly at Welch, "We'll give you guys $100 bucks a day plus all the fares you can grab from the airport. All you guys have to do is push out those blue and white assholes. How you do it is your business." Since the lease guys were a rough bunch to start with, this was turning out to be a gold mine for them.

It took three months, but blue and white left after being turned into black and blue. Not only did Paul rake in big bucks during the "taxi wars," but he also got his settlement check and purchased five brand new taxicabs of his own. Welch provided the drivers, and they were in business. Some legit, some not so legit. Paul finally stopped driving altogether and started investing his profits into buying more cars, and eventually, adding taxis for the handicapped, vans with hydraulic lifts, an idea he got from Bobby Ray's transportation predicaments. Ironically, he also got into the airport business, using the same tactics that helped the owner company get rid of the upstarts. By 1978, he was a millionaire. He dabbled in political intrigue, as it was the lifeblood of a capitol city like Albany. Ultimately becoming a ward leader for the Irish/Black section of the city.

He married a bookkeeper who he had hired, and they had four lovely kids. Two boys and two girls. Looked like the

American dream. As Paul stayed off the booze and only looked forward instead of backward, things were groovy. But the past kept smothering, and Paul tried private psychotherapy to deal with it. After ten years they divorced amicably. They never argued, and Paul took care of all the financial aspects of their lives. He took his kids out regularly and, by all accounts, was as good a dad as he could be.

The problem was defined by his analyst as this: by staying drunk or busy or gambling or whoring or politicking or working hard, Paul was deferring his resolution as to what had happened previously in his life. It was about time to think and deal with it, like it or not. So, in 1998 he backtracked as best he could. This led to his decision to reacquaint himself with Bobby Ray Jackson.

He called several numbers in the Spartanburg metro area, which included Gaffney, for Jackson, hitting pay dirt on his fifth try. He reached a woman who paused for a minute after he had stated, "I'm looking to get in touch with Bobby Ray Jackson the third, who I was in the Army with in 1967."

"Bobby Ray from Gaffney?"

"Yes, yes, the football player, he became a paratrooper."

"Who is this, please?"

"Paul Fogarty from New York. I was a good friend of Bobby Ray's."

"Are you that skinny boy from New York that Bobby Ray used to bring down here on the weekends?"

"Yes, Mrs. Jackson, that was me, except I'm not so skinny now," Paul kidded. Another pause, and finally, she reported, "I'm afraid Bobby Ray passed. Been a couple of years now. He spoke of you often, felt bad about losing contact with you. I think he was a little embarrassed about the prison situation."

Paul was struck silent, finally forcing himself to realize that, of course, this was the only realistic scenario that could have come about. He recovered after a few seconds. "I'm so sorry, Mrs. Jackson. I truly hoped to get in touch with him again and see how things were going."

She told her tale matter-of-factly. "The drink got to him, and he was always thinking about the war. I can only hope, and I pray to the Almighty Father every day, that he is finally at peace."

Then Paul quickly said, without really thinking it through, "I'd like to come and visit his gravesite, soon, if that would be possible."

She was pleased with this. "Oh, of course, you must come and see his daughter Charlene. She still lives in the area. His other daughter, Rona, was killed in a car accident just last year. They are buried next to each other, along with his dad, who also passed."

Paul commiserated, "Oh my God, how very sad for you and Charlene." Paul got the address for Mrs. Jackson and the phone number and address for Charlene. Soon as he started planning his trip to South Carolina.

He was still numb when he hung up. But he didn't cry. He wasn't much into the crying jag yet. He would get more proficient at this as time progressed. Looking at his calendar, he decided to go down to South Carolina next week. Before he left, though, he rifled through his old Army photos and found several of himself with Bobby Ray and some shots of Bobby Ray alone. They were both fond of posing with rifles, bayonets and camouflage painted faces, looking as sinister as possible at the Kodak instamatic. In reality, the pictures looked like kids. Big kids playing at war, but still kids, nonetheless. He packed the photos, and he packed Bobby Ray's favorite black Johnny Cash type dress shirt, which Bobby Ray left behind, and Paul could never bring himself to toss. This was the beginning of the pilgrimage to his past, and unknowingly to his immediate future.

He got off the plane in Spartanburg, South Carolina and rented an SUV from Hertz. Remembering the mud around Bobby Ray's parents' trailer, he figured he might need some four-wheeled driving help, especially if it rained. He was damned good at preparing for most contingencies.

When he got to Gaffney, he didn't remember anything about the center of town. But then again, it was daylight, and he and Bobby Ray never went to downtown in the daytime. At least not that he could remember. He called Mrs. Jackson, and she said that Charlene was on her way over, and gave him good directions as to how to get to them. It was a cloudy day, but the sun was trying to break through, and Paul was looking at the sundogs. He couldn't help but think that maybe it was a sign from up high that Bobby Ray, wherever his spirit lay, was aware of this journey and was letting him know that he approved.

Paul always had a marked fascination with sundogs, ever since noticing them for the first time on a hill overlooking PS #20 in North Albany. He thought at the time that God was signaling him. And, ironically, that evening, he pitched a no-hit, no-run game for his little league team, Hermie's Garage. He was a believer after that. When he saw sundogs once in West Germany, while standing around looking for chicks at the concentration camp museum, they seemed to point to the crematorium. He ruminated on that for a while, but never really figured out what God was trying to indicate with the sign. Probably wasn't meant for him. Kind of like a party line thing.

Maybe it was for the Jewish nuns.

He pulled off the road and parked in front of the mobile home. The skirt around the base was detached in a few places, and the ramp was new, but Paul recognized the place. The difference was that there were no old cars scattered around the property as Bobby Ray's dad was always fixing them up for repair or resale. What was most familiar to him was the smell. It was a smell of pine needles and red clay, and it brought him back in time. It seemed to Paul that he had two triggers that he had to be careful about that could bring him back to the booze, music—consciously—and smells—unconsciously.

This specific aroma caused instant melancholy. Not a déjà vu type feeling, but more of an omnipresent blanket of nostalgia mixed with depression. He embraced the feeling. Paul embraced any feeling that seemed to come spontaneously, especially if it brought him face to face with his psyche. He took a few minutes to breathe, knowing instinctively that what he was doing right now was, indeed, the right thing to do. This was the first stage of the final penance of his life. He was at peace with that. It seemed like he was in the tally process of his existence. His tale had to be told—told to himself, by himself. He also planned to leave Charlene and Mrs. Jackson a carton. Inside were pictures of Bobby Ray, a black Johnny Cash type shirt, and a certified check for $40,000. He would ask them to open the carton only after he had pulled away. His reason to them for leaving the package to be opened after his departure was that he didn't want to cry in front of them. Paul was always planning. Attention to detail was one of his strongest assets. Fact was, he figured he still had a little guilt about Bobby Ray's fate. Maybe he could have done something different back in Albany. Maybe he should have tough-loved him. Maybe, *shoulda, coulda, woulda, fuck it.*

When Paul saw Mrs. Jackson, he thought he wouldn't have recognized her if he saw her downtown. He looked carefully to see if there was any sign of Bobby Ray in her face, but nope. Nada. Her daughter Charlene was in her 30's, natural blond, a little on the heavy side, but not bad. She was compact, like Bobby Ray, and Paul could definitely see the resemblance. They invited Paul in and were both staring at him, uncomfortably. Mrs. Jackson, trying to remember the skinny kid from New York, and Charlene, conjuring up thoughts about her dad's friend, hoping for a tidbit that perhaps Bobby Ray had confided to this stranger his love for the little girl he left behind.

"If memory serves me right, peach pie was your favorite. I made two of them for you, one to eat here and one for the road," said Mrs. Jackson. "And if you like, I have written down the recipe for you up there in New York."

Paul smiled, "Mrs. Jackson, how thoughtful of you. I've never tasted peach pie even remotely as good as yours, and believe me, I have tasted peach pies from all over. Yours is one of a kind. I thank you and God bless you."

Small talk aside, Paul had a sweetened iced tea and two slices of peach pie, with a side of vanilla ice cream. Furnishings were adequate but spare and worn. Mrs. Jackson looked tired, ready to give up the ghost sooner rather than later. Both ladies smoked, though they did ask Paul if he minded. He said, "Of course not," but he did.

Mrs. Jackson pulled out a couple of well-worn photo albums and a grainy 8mm film showing Bobby Ray at a family gathering in 1990. He was surprised that they still had a film projector using 8mm. *How old was that thing?* Color was good, though. Bobby Ray had gained some weight, and his face was lined and flaccid. He still had the booming voice though and sang some of "Folsom Prison Blues" for the gathering. Wasn't a bad rendition either. You could tell the singer was enjoying himself.

Paul was watching this film on the living room wall with the feeling of an interloper almost. The cast on the wall kind of reminded him of the barroom crowds, speaking wreckese, only with a southern white-trashy type accent. Charlene pointed out her sister Rona, a shapely brunette who stood together, holding hands with a guy sporting a mullet, naturally. The crew in the film could have been stand-ins for a James Dickey novel.

Pictures viewed, 8mm done, one peach pie eaten and the remaining one wrapped in aluminum foil, Paul made his announcement.

"Mrs. Jackson and Charlene, I have a carton here with a few photos of Bobby Ray, his favorite shirt that he gave to me, and a small gift for you in remembrance of my friend. I only ask that you wait until I have left before you open the carton as I'm afraid I get rather sad and sentimental seeing those things again. I hope you understand."

"Sure thing, Paul," Mrs. Jackson said.

Charlene offered, "Want to go up to the graveyard to see Daddy?"

He bade Mrs. Jackson good-bye, secretly forgiving her for her "Yankee Boy" remark thirty years prior. He kissed her cheek, hugged her, and said thank you and God Bless—he always felt like Red Skelton as Freddie the Freeloader when he said God bless—looking into her eyes as they both knew she would soon be dead. As would he.

Charlene insisted on driving, so she and Paul hopped in her VW Rabbit—Bobby Ray II would not have approved of the Kraut car for his granddaughter—and drove the seven miles to the cemetery. No chatter en route. Paul had his sunglasses on and felt protected by them. *Dammit,* no sundogs. That would have been so cool.

Bobby Ray III and Bobby Ray II had identical military headstones. *Robert Raymond Jackson II, WWII, T/Sgt, US Army, 1923-1973* alongside *Robert Raymond Jackson III, Viet Nam, Sgt, US Army, Purple Heart, Silver Star Medal, 1946-1996.* To the rear of these was a small headstone marked *Rona Jackson Denton, beloved wife and daughter, RIP 1967-1997.*

Bobby Ray III out-cocked Bobby Ray II in the headstone competition. He would have been pleased. Probably the only one to notice the distinction was the man now standing in front of the graves. And maybe a couple of the guys from the local VFW.

Paul got on his knees and prayed in front of III's stone. He blessed himself with the sign of the cross and said his usual litany, an Our Father, A Hail Mary, A Glory Be, wrapped up with an Act of Contrition, on behalf of the dead guy. He was a daily praying guy, for the last twenty-seven years anyway. A smattering of saints to fit the occasion. In this case, St. Maurice, patron saint of warriors; St. Joseph, family man icon; and St. Francis of Assisi, saint of inner peace and love for nature. He just kind of threw that last one in because he didn't know who the patron saint of NASCAR was. Then, he silently reached into his pocket and pulled out an ancient inhaler, a puffer for asthmatics. He had found it in his apartment while cleaning up a few years back, knew immediately where it came from, and, like the shirt, couldn't shed it. Paul placed it on the top of the headstone and said to himself—and to Bobby Ray—softly, "I miss you, buddy. I'm sorry I wasn't there for you. I love you, man." Standing erect, he transformed himself into a younger man, forty years younger, and saluted. Charlene watched all this with tears in her eyes. He finished his hand salute, did an about-face, and hugged Charlene for a long time. Though he didn't cry, he choked up a little. They walked over, arms around each other, and sat on a small bench.

Charlene was the first to speak. "Didn't really know him. I tried to know him, but he was a private person, even to his daughters. But I think I know that he loved me. I'm sure he loved both of us." It dawned on Paul that Charlene was looking for reassurance as he could be perceptive when his antennae were up. He didn't want to go over the top, knowing that the words he was about to speak would stay with this woman for what was left of her life, so they should be chosen and spoken carefully. Not that he had any compunction about lying, just wanted the words to be right. Bobby Ray couldn't get the words right for her, so maybe Paul could. He started, "I shouldn't say this Charlene, but I must. Most parents won't admit it, but they do have favorites. Doesn't mean they love the other children less. They just have favorites. Human nature. Bobby Ray used to feel guilty when he'd talk to me about you. You were his favorite. He wanted you to know how much he loved you, and he was fearful that the war had drained all the love out of him. He also thought that you would feel sorry for him because of his wounds. I tried to tell him that wasn't the case, but he was convinced."

She was startled. "Oh, my goodness. Never, never. I loved my Daddy. He had the nicest smile. He used to drive me and Rona around in this big old green sports car. We'd get ice cream and such, go to the drive-in. He was so nice to us. He made us feel like we were special."

"Well," Paul went on, "you girls were his reason for living, and especially you, Charlene. I know your dad would want you to know that." He did feel a smidgen of guilt when he glanced over at Rona's marker. Charlene leaned over and hugged him tightly for a long time. Paul looked up in the sky, hoping to see a sundog or a mini sundog, but no luck.

The two survivors were related by the time they got back into the Rabbit. Paul knew he did right. *God Bless.*

Chapter 14

Return to the Whisky-A-Go-Go (Not the real one)

Paul woke with a start. He was disoriented at first but, hearing the hum of the space heater in the rural motel, he fell back into an easy, relaxed semi-slumber. Physically, he was still in Kathy's hometown, but mentally, he was remembering the rest of the trip in '98, after going to the three Jackson's graves.

Charlene dropped Paul off at his car at Mrs. Jackson's place. Charlene had told him about Bobby Ray's girlfriend, Lu-Anna, who worked at the post office. Paul decided to take a trip downtown to the post office and try to at least see her, get a sense, and maybe engage in a conversation. He headed down to W. Floyd Baker Boulevard and found the building, parked, and walked in. It was a good-sized building, so he approached the attendants, both male. He went up to the older of the two and said, "Hi, I'm looking for Lu-Anna. Does she still work here?" His Yankee accent and leather jacket said New York all over. Naturally, the worker was a little suspicious.

"Do you mean Lu-Anna Davis?" asked the worker.

Paul didn't know the last name, never asked Charlene for it. *How many Lu-Anna's could be working here in the post office,* he thought. "Yes, that's her," said Paul.

"Hold on, she's in the back, I'll get her for you. Could I get your name, please?"

"My name is Paul Fogarty from New York. I was in the Army with Bobby Ray Jackson." Paul stared straight at the man, and it seemed to do the trick as he went back, and the patriot got Lu-Anna.

Paul saw a tall woman, bleach blond and teased hair sticking up from a visor. You could tell she was a looker back in the day. She moved fast, appeared to be an energetic person. "How can I help you, sir?" she asked, with that southern saccharin smile. Paul stated his case and asked if she had a break or something coming up so they could get a coffee and maybe a few minutes of her time to talk about Bobby Ray. She said, "I get off at three. Come on over to the diner across the street, and we can talk."

As it was 2:10 now, Paul readily agreed. He walked down the boulevard, looking in some shop windows. He found a jewelry store that looked promising, went in and bought a delicate cameo watch for his ex-wife. She really liked watches, and she was a good mother to the kids. Never asking him many questions about things past, she was pleasant, and the kids were crazy about her. Paul thought that she probably never loved him but felt comfortable and secure around him. Like most women did. She never saw the drunken side of him. If she did, she wouldn't have stuck around.

Paul was already seated at a booth in the diner when Lu-Anna Davis came in, still wearing her visor. He waved her over, and she sat. Paul said, "I took the liberty of ordering a coffee for you. Can I interest you in some dinner or perhaps a pastry?"

"Well, thank you, that was thoughtful. I'll just sip the coffee. I really must be getting home soon. Tonight, I go to my exercise group."

"I wanted to talk about Bobby Ray. He was my friend. We'd been through a lot together, and I just recently discovered his death."

"Well, Bobby Ray and I were living together down around Spartanburg for a while. We got on nice, and he needed me increasingly. He was so sick the last year of his life. I think he knew he was dying, but he didn't seem to have much will left if you know what I mean. He smoked all the time, which was nasty with his asthma condition and all. And, truth be told, he let the drink get hold of him, even when those VA doctors said it was destroying his liver. He laughed it off, said it relaxed him. He couldn't even really drive down to the VFW hall after a while. Just had me pick up some liquor at the package store and bring it home."

Paul asked, "Did he talk about the war or the army much?"

"Not really," said Lu-Anna. "Sometimes, when he was in his cups, he would say some, but it wasn't like he talked about it all the time. But I think it was always on his mind. He used to sit in the sun on the back deck, and he would just stare out toward the trees. I think that he was pretty much convinced that he should have died over there. Was probably the reason he didn't care too much about life. He did love his mama and baby girls, though. And he was kind to my son, who was a teenager then. When Bobby Ray was well enough, he'd take him fishing and to the car races and such. Showed him things to fix up his car. Bobby Ray was a good man. A sad man, but a good one."

Again, Paul was at a loss for words and was starting to feel as if he was intruding on all these people. But it seemed Bobby Ray's mother, paramour, and Charlene, his daughter, were happy to share their feelings and stories to him. Charlene felt that thing that the self-proclaimed experts define as "closure." But Paul didn't know or sense this and felt a little bit like a voyeur. He felt like he was part of a script. It was ironic that Paul always felt comfortable around black guys and deeply felt equal, but around these white southerners, he felt superior. On reflection, it dawned on Paul that it was himself that was prejudiced. This was a shocker to Paul, but it was an honest and an absolute truth. If he learned nothing else down here in SC, he had discovered this side of himself. Instantly he was making conscious attempts to amend his previously thought of innate leanings of contempt and antipathy toward these people. This was a remarkable illustration to Paul that he learned something about himself down here, and he was determined not to waste this knowledge. He couldn't wait to get home to tell his buddies of what he had learned. Further, it hit him, maybe Bobby Ray had somehow sensed Paul's prejudice. Maybe he tried to show Paul, consciously or not, that Paul was just as prejudiced against the people who didn't share his values as Paul smugly assumed every southerner was against blacks.

This was a major revelation and one that stopped Paul in his tracks. Unfortunately, he hadn't heard a word that Lu-Anna had said in the last few minutes but recovered enough to smile and bid her adieu with sincerity for her help in his quest. She left the booth, and Paul sat there for another twenty minutes, considering the ramifications of his newly discovered frailty.

As soon as he left the diner, he started on the road to Columbus, GA. He didn't think about getting a motel, just figured he'd start driving the 300-miles to Fort Benning now and sleep when he got tired. Paul had a lot to think about on the trip. For one thing, maybe getting the SUV at the car rental wasn't the way to go for a long haul like this. *Oh well*, thought Paul, *I spent a lot of hours in taxicabs on my ass that were a lot more uncomfortable.* He started to get a little bit of the highway hypnosis on I-85 South while looking at the trucks and buses belching smoke north and south. His only job was to monitor his thoughts and keep his foot near the brake pedal since he had the car on cruise control. He didn't turn the heater on, fearing it would make him sleepy, but he had removed his leather jacket for comfort driving and because he liked the feeling of being a little chilly in the car. That helped to keep him awake. No radio either. Couldn't find any soul or R&B. Hated country, and oldies. Again, the thought cropped up, *are my musical tastes a sign of my newly discovered prejudice?*

Coffee, piss, and gas stops were united into a single task. Only making two of them en route, he arrived in Columbus, just outside the fort, at 11:30PM. He drove down Victory Drive, toward the main gate, looking for a motel. There were plenty of these, as well as tattoo parlors, pawnshops, fast food joints, military regalia shops, laundries, tailors, barbers, and barrooms. New and used car dealerships also displayed patriotic-chromed, macho themes to entice the young warriors located nearby. This was the surreal gauntlet that haunted the main drags into and out of every large military base in the country. It also had not changed in forty years as far as Paul was concerned, except for computer/electronic stores added to the mix.

Paul booked a Super 8 and dropped his suitcase off. He drove down to a Denny's and ordered a Grand Slam breakfast. The place was jumping with soldiers, loud, some drunk, some ornately tattooed and all male troopers sporting the "high and tight" haircuts of the elite warrior, while the Red-Hot Chili Peppers wailed on the juke. Paul kept his eyes open and mouth shut because when he closed his eyes, his mind was instantly transported to the same restaurant, hearing the same voices of thirty years past.

He got a huge lump in his throat, and tears came to his eyes. A lot of these voices seemed attached to memories of the dead and wounded of his war. At the very least, they were reminders of young, healthy men who blindly followed their orders to their peril. Those that were still alive, like Paul, were sentenced to dream and hear the voices of the lost … forever.

My God, thought Paul, *were we that young? Were we that carefree? Didn't we realize what was coming?* Jesus said, "Father, let this cup pass from me." *We didn't, why?* Jesus also said, "But Your will, not mine be done." *We didn't, we just went.* Except maybe Posie—he knew what was coming. He went anyway. Paul thought of several guys who knew before they went that they weren't coming home. And they were right. But still, they went. Was this courage? Was this insanity? *Where was God in all of this?*

Did Charley have a restaurant like this where the NVA and VC partied and ate before they also went to their doom? Paul was overwhelmed. He didn't expect this. This was one time where he was not happy about coming face to face with his psyche. Boldly, stupidly, he had walked back into the belly of the beast. He had to get out of here right away. He almost ran to his car. Staring from his car for almost an hour, he looked at these poor doomed kids. Whether they lived or died, they were doomed. If only he could tell them.

When he finally broke away from the restaurant, he was too rattled to sleep, so he drove aimlessly down Victory Way searching for, *what*, he didn't know. He got off on 10th Ave and started north on this route, feeling a little bit of familiarity. Paul wanted to find the Whisky-A-Go-Go—not the real one. It was probably long gone by now, but he wanted to see what became of the building and, perchance, to go inside.

His mind slipped back to the night that he and Bobby Ray went down there after Bobby Ray received his Viet Nam orders. The music was blaring, and he could remember Mitch Ryder and the Detroit Wheels playing "Devil with a Blue Dress" on the jukebox. Bobby Ray had to yell at him to be heard above the cacophony of "yee-haa's" from the grits. The joint was so crowded you had to push your way through to get to the bar. It was on that night that a huge, contagious fight lit up and then spread, like a house fire, throughout the property. The bouncers started tossing G.I.'s around like they were rice at a wedding. Paul and Bobby Ray got caught up in it and took their shots as deemed responsive and appropriate. Paul felt no fear during this. Maybe it was the alcohol, or maybe it was the training he had recently gone through, but he just reacted. As did Bobby Ray, with the requisite password, "yee-haa, motherfucker."

At the apex of the brawl, someone fired a glass. It broke against the wall. Bad move, for now, glasses, chairs, and even a table became airborne amongst the airborne. Now the injuries were getting serious. Paul got hit in the shoulder with a shot glass, and he picked it up from the floor and tossed it in the direction from whence it came. He could throw hard. It hit an older bouncer named Nick, a former army ranger, smack dab in the left eye. Nick doubled over in shock and agony, eye socket bleeding profusely. Paul saw the whole thing, as if in slow motion. Nick was out of the fight, but he didn't know where the glass came from.

Finally, the Columbus PD and Army MP's came in and busted some skulls with billy clubs and jacks, ending the fight and closing the bar. On his way, being pushed out of the bar, Paul looked at Nick, still doubled over. Blood filled Nick's huge left hand, which cupped the eye. Paul met Bobby Ray outside, who was sporting a huge knot in the center of his forehead. They laughed like hell and ran down to the bus station to catch a bus back to the Fort.

The next day, the Columbus Ledger-Enquirer, on page one of the local news announced, "WAITER LOSES EYE IN BAR FIGHT." The only reason Paul saw it was because Posie showed him the paper and asked if he ever had gone to the Whisky-A-Go-Go. Paul said, "I was in there once. It sucked." But he read the article thoroughly and immediately felt queasy. He went back to his bunk and lay down and shook. Paul thought, *did anybody see me throw it? Will they investigate and catch me? Oh, my God.* He never said a word to anyone about this incident. Never once did he feel any remorse for throwing the glass, only fear of getting caught. Even now, he didn't feel bad for Nick. *Fuck Nick.*

Paul couldn't find any reminders of the bar and wasn't sure if he was even on the right street. But his memory did stir. And that was what he came here for.

And unbeknownst to Paul, three years after this brawl, Nick the waiter shot himself in his right eye. The suicide was not reported in the paper. It just said he died suddenly. But he really was one of the soldiers who died of a long-wasting disease called *nobody gives a fuck.*

Paul drove back to the motel and slept soundly. The demons didn't come that night. The demons had a long day and were exhausted. *God Bless.*

Chapter 15

The Woods are lovely, dark, and deep ...

Back in Cattaraugus County, Paul got up the next morning at about 11:00AM, showered, and paid his tab. He didn't want to charge the room to his credit card as he knew this would create a bill that would never be paid. And Paul, all things considered, was an honest guy who paid strict attention to detail. He had paid all his bills to date.

He was leaving an estate worth well over four million dollars, making sure that he left two hundred thousand dollars to the Albany Boy's Club, or as it was now known, the Albany Boy's and Girl's Club. If it weren't for the Boy's Club, Paul wouldn't have had a place to go when he was walking the streets. He even went back to the Boy's Club when he was discharged from the Army at age ninteen. He liked to shoot hoops. Eventually, the manager of the club told Paul he was too old to come anymore as a member, and that he should join the Y. Paul was disappointed, but he and his buddy Bernie, who was twenty-two years old and was playing basketball too, accepted their fate. Apparently, they were scaring the younger kids. They didn't join the Y, they just shot hoops at the park where the streetlights were on all night. The Boy's Club was home to a lot of the kids who had no place to go. But that is a different story.

Paul's mind was racing in a lot of different directions now. There would be no more delays. This was the day. He wasn't afraid, and it felt as if each event was automatically pushing him to the last act of this play. He was calm, clear headed, and amazingly, incredibly hungry. Maybe this was just a subconscious stall for time before the rest of the days' events unfolded, but he knew better. He was resolute. Stopping at MacDonald's, he got a big breakfast—Sausage-english muffin, pancakes, hashbrowns. No sense worrying about cholesterol now. After breakfast, he headed up the road to the cemetery. He planned on spending hours there, some of them while he was still alive.

It was just after noon when he pulled into the cemetery. He had looked on the internet and found the website for the graveyard and electronically located the grave he was looking for. Today it was sunny and unusually warm for a winter's day. The snow was starting to melt, and little rivers of water fought their way down slopes and into puddles. He loved the smell of the warm mud that portended the coming of spring. Not a cloud in the sky.

Paul pondered, *cemeteries are the most peaceful of places.* Any season brought solitude and comfort to the living. Paul thought about his father's gravesite back in Troy, New York. It was a Catholic church cemetery, and the graves were not kept up well, despite the "perpetual care" markers on them. Just a sales pitch, probably. Except for the nun's graves. They were buried in a community style, much like they lived their lives, and the caretakers knew that the grass had better be trimmed always because the sisters' graves got a steady stream of visitors. One of the things Paul noticed at the Troy graveyard was its proximity to an elementary school. When he visited his dad's grave, he could sometimes hear the kids playing and yelling. He figured that dad would have liked that. Paul didn't think too much about Dad's or his own corpse decomposing in its grave. Even if the best embalmers of all time preserved it, it would have to rot sometime. But he didn't like the idea of cremation. He had no reason for this, just thought it was a little like getting rid of refuse. He might be laying in a box, in a vault, rotting away, but dammit, at least there would be some trace of his mortal ass for some time. Whatever good that was. It occurred to Paul that when you had a tooth pulled, you didn't care what happened to the tooth. It was just a hunk of rotted ivory and Capsin that wasn't even noticeable for all the pain it caused before its extraction. Kind of like the body, after the pain of cancer, gunshots, heart disease, or whatever. Pain envelopes. You endure. You die. He also wondered if Bobby Ray and his unfortunate companions felt the same about their missing limbs, laying on the battlefield or on the surgical floor, as he did about his tooth.

Probably a good analogy but not a fair comparison.

His memory slipped back to one night in New York when he was working his huckle in the cab on a hot summer night, about four A.M. He was listening to his cassette player, Doobies—*China Grove* when he noticed, far too late, a Labrador retriever sitting in the middle of the street, tongue out, happy and content. Paul saw the creature too late to react, with his constantly diminished capacity caused by alcohol, and he hit the dog. He could feel the head of the dog hit his front axle. Boom, watermelon dropped on pavement. He stopped, got out, walked back, and looked at the canine's severely twisted body. Tongue still out, blood mixed with the saliva. The dog twitched a couple of times and was then still.

Paul ran back to his cab and said some prayers for the dog. He really felt terrible, but he tried to put it into perspective. *It's a friggen dog, for Christ's sake.* But he knew, in his inner soul, that if he were sober and paying attention, Fido would still be kicking. Lesson learned? None. Put another black mark on his bad side. But these were starting to add up, and the dog was a big factor in Paul's decision to get sober. So maybe Lassie did not die in vain. Or at least this sign from the netherworld was working as it was supposed to.

He found the grave he was looking for. *Kathryn Urbanski, 1946-1973, Beloved wife and daughter.* In small scrolling at the base of the stone, hardly noticeable, *"The woods are lovely, dark and deep ... "* Parking his car on top of a non-occupied mound, he got out and opened the trunk. After unwrapping the Mossberg, adjustable choke shotgun, he examined it. He placed the weapon atop the blanket still in the trunk and got the box of shells out, laying them alongside the gun. Taking one slug out, he chambered the round and slammed the receiver home. Having loaded it, he laid the weapon on the blanket, wrapped it, and closed the trunk, leaving the key in the lock for rapid retrieval. He was almost ready for the ritual but got in the passenger side of the car and looked out at the rest of the graveyard. Amazingly, the cemetery was much as he pictured it would look on his arrival. Paul's projections were always reliable, or at least he thought they were.

Paul didn't count on the physical manifestations on his body from the psychological impetus of his potential act. *Although everyone must die, he thought, no one really believes that their time is up.* Even a condemned man thinks the Governor will call on the hot line at the last minute. It's just human nature. To make a conscious decision to end one's own life, to be the instrument of one's own demise, must be one of two things: either an act of desperation and insanity or the purest and noblest act of contrition and love. Paul, only recently, in the last year or so, believed in the latter. His disjointed Roman Catholic upbringing would not let him consider suicide for himself or for anyone. It was anathema to take the life away that God Himself had given you. But the journey had taken Paul too far. The time had finally come for Paul to look at self-destruction in a different light. Had the lessons all been learned? Was it time to "cash in and go home?" Would Paul consign himself to never ending agony for taking that which was not his to take?

He thought about the saints. None of them committed suicide. But the stories of the saints were legion in the way that they set themselves up for death by martyrdom. Was this the same? Dying for Christ? They had obviously made the fatal decision to give their lives, some probably for eternal bliss. Others, for the love of the Savior in which they heartily believed. What was the difference? Paul thought, *what is the difference in their conscious decision to die and mine? Because they were put to death by their persecutors? Aren't my trials and torments the result of my persecutors in life?* Was this another rationalization for him, and on and on?

He owed this to Kathy. He owed this to Bobby Ray. He owed this to Jesus. Paul must pay for his sins of commission, but more so for his ignorance and sins of omission. Concentrating on each word, he started his Act of Contrition. "Oh my God, I am heartily sorry for having offended Thee, and I detest all my sins because I dread the loss of heaven and the pains of hell but most of all because I have offended Thee, my Lord ... Who art all good and deserving of all my love. I firmly resolve, with the help of Thy grace, to confess my sins, do penance and to amend my life ... Amen."

The last three letters in "amend" are "end." Amen—d. I *am en*ding in good faith.

The only contradiction appeared to be the "amend my life part," thought Paul. Is killing yourself an amendment? Or should this prayer, at least for Paul, for now, end with just the do penance part? Paul believed in the axiom that prayer was just conversation with God that was scripted. He was changing the script a little, which he believed was his right.

To do penance, that's why Paul was here. What greater penance for a selfish coward than to put a shotgun in his mouth? What greater show of love for a woman she thought was unrequited because of ignorance and alcohol? What greater thanks for being allowed to walk on this earth for fifty-nine years on two good legs? To hold his children in two good arms. No, Paul was committed. He was also frightened but thought that was a good thing. To not be scared would be a sign of insanity, even though he assumed all would think him so after his death. They would probably even have the clergy assume him insane so that his mortal remains, headless as they would be, could be implanted in consecrated ground. Paul knew he would not back down from this act. It was, after all, he now believed, not a sin, but indeed, a sacred event. Atonement for the people he had hurt. And recompense for the gifts he had received. It was, in a word, justice. No more, no less. End of debate. Time for a final, pure reflection. Time for undistorted communion with the spirits that, Paul believed, would soon be welcoming him to their aura and abode. Almost time to die.

Chapter 16

There's a crazy man up here!

As Paul sat there gazing, thinking, he felt a sudden sense of tranquility and oneness with the spirit world. To Paul, it seemed a visceral quake from deep inside. He knew something was happening, was guiding him, taking control of his thoughts and feelings. It was splendid. In his mind, he sensed colors that were amazing and indescribable. Reds of the deepest, warmest hue, the color of venous blood crowning waves of flowers gently swaying with a wind that you could see as well as feel. A mass of different and gorgeous shades of greenish capillary-like webs, moving in a continuous panorama. Was this the stress reaction? Was this a preview of the world to come? He had no fear, just awe, and felt a kinship with this spirit—and a love. A love that he had never experienced before. Pure, complete, omnipotent.

He sensed Kathy's hand on his shoulder. Imagining her hand gently stroking the nape of his neck and reaching to muss up his hair. He didn't fight it but went with it.

Wherever this had come from, he cared not. He wasn't going to let it go. Blindly, willingly, and happily, he was traipsing over to the other side. *Thank you, thank you, Lord, for bringing me here. Thank you for letting me feel, really feel for the first time ever.*

Flashback to a hospital room in the old section of Albany Medical Center Hospital. It was four o'clock in the morning, winter 1971. A tall, skinny drunk man took the elevator from the basement to the fourth floor. He got out, turned right, and then left, opened the door to K-407 and saw a young woman, intubated, IV'd, and EKG'd. The light cast upon her by the parking lot floods was eerily reminiscent of a still motion black-light show.

Her long, almost black hair was splayed on the pillow as she lay, supine, being artificially ventilated. A fallen angel with a heart monitor.

The tall, drunk man sat on the plastic chair next to her bed and whispered, "Kathy, I am here. I love you. More than anything, I want you to get better." He reached into the side pocket of his canvas work jacket and withdrew a can of Schaefer's. Popping the top, he tossed it toward the wastebasket and put his feet up, work boots and all, on the foot of her bed. He drank a couple of swallows of beer and almost fell asleep, feeling good like a sentinel. The woman that was laying there could feel his thoughts as he conveyed them in her direction, he sensed. In fact, he knew she could.

The tall, skinny drunk man ESP'd his love to the patient. He knew she received the transmission—he could feel it. Mentally, he fired, "I'm sorry I moved out when you were at work, and for sleeping with everyone in sight, and for drinking myself into a coma every day and night, and for not holding you closely when you were scared, and for not living up to my potential."

The tall, skinny man was truly sorry for all these and more. But he knew he couldn't change them. She was probably going to die, either now or soon after. He didn't lose her, rather, had given her up, let her go. It was the biggest mistake of his life. The tall, skinny drunk named Paul already felt as if he had forsaken, not only this lovely girl but himself as well.

The dawn started coming up, parking lot lights went out, and Paul got out of the chair slowly and kissed Kathy on her sleeping forehead. He thought he saw a tear in her left eye, which to him confirmed his transference techniques of barely an hour past. He slugged down the remnant of his now warm beer, belched, and left the room. As he was walking toward the elevator, a nurse with a med cart and an inordinate amount of starch in her uniform with that obnoxious little cap challenged him.

"Hey, who are you and what the hell are you doing here?"

Paul, mustering up as much dignity as a tall, skinny drunk man could, responded, perhaps unwisely, "Go fuck yourself, tight-assed bitch."

He then belched loudly and farted, almost shitting himself in the process. Feeling smug, he pushed the elevator button, got in the car, and rode to the basement.

The nurse was on the house phone to security in a flash. "There's a crazy man up here. He just took the elevator in K Building and, wait … yes, he's stopped in the basement. He smells like a brewery, and I think he came from a patient's room."

At the same time, Paul stepped out of the elevator and started for the tunnel that led to the way out. Two uniformed security guards came running after him, just as he made his way into the fresh air. "Stop! Stop!" one yelled.

Paul turned around. "Or what? You'll roll on me? You fat fucks!"

They charged and got him on the ground on his belly. Unbelievably, they cuffed him with plastic handcuffs. Paul said, "Okay, Porky, ya got me." He could have been a little more diplomatic. The wannabe police officers grabbed his arms and twisted him to an upright position. They rousted him to their little security office and then called the nurse upstairs to come down and identify him. *It appears,* thought Paul, *in their minds that there must be several drunk men walking around the hospital at five-thirty in the morning,* and these diligent officers wanted to make sure they had the right one. Nurse Ratched appeared and pointed her finger, which also looked like it might have been starched.

"He's the one!"

J'accuse, busted, abandon all hope. Paul busted out laughing.

Meanwhile, one of the wannabe gendarmes grabbed his wallet. When he searched it, he saw the paratrooper wings tacked to the inside. He said to Paul, "Are you airborne?"

Paul said, "Not at the moment."

"Don't be a wise-ass, what's going on?"

"I was visiting my girlfriend."

Dick Tracy said, "What's her name?"

When Paul had given them all the information, and they were assured that the patient was not molested and nothing was missing, they decided to let him go with a sermon. The motivation for his release had nothing to do with Paul being an ex-paratrooper, but everything to do with the fact that these two guys were getting off in a half-hour. And Dan-Dee Donuts opened at six. They also realized that they had probably violated several laws in the apprehension, not the least of which was taking his wallet without permission. Paul was silent, acted penitent, and was released with a stern warning.

He forgot about this entire incident until just now.

Now he knew that Kathy was aware of his presence on that night and she pulled through because of it. Now. Would she have still pulled through down the road if he had come back into her life? Now, he had no choice. He had to face this before he met her spirit.

Or, more correctly, he had to try to figure out the mortal answer as the immortal answer would soon come. He cried, tears coming from his left eye, cold and neutral.

Chapter 17

The Whorehouse

A half-hour passed. At the cemetery, Paul was getting a little chilly, so he tried to turn the car's heater on. *Where are the keys?* Checked his pockets, floor, and dashboards. No luck. Well, they're just going to have to tow it away from here when his ass was discovered. He got out of the car to look on the ground for the keys, and it dawned on him ... the trunk. *I left them in the trunk so I could get the gun quickly, hurry to the grave, and complete the mission.* He grabbed them and started the car and heater. *Okay, get it together,* thought Paul, *stop the bullshit.*

Just like the hospital incident, another pulse wave of memories hit him hard. Again, part of this was a first, though the rest was a private memory. He was embarrassed to relate this story to anybody. That same power must have brought the new memory to him. It was like he was being forced to recall, in detail, the events of the afternoon in question. It was in Kathy's rented house. It was winter. Man, it was always winter. It was cold out and gray. Not cloudy, more like being in a cloud. Her bedroom was in the front of the house, and the house only had one floor. They were in bed, having been out all night till five, deciding to sleep in. The shades were down, but there was plenty of light. Paul had his arms around a naked, smiling Kathy. They eased into making love. Paul was on top, and she had her eyes closed but was smiling and holding him as one.

She threw her arms back under her head and was feeling good. Her eyes still closed, Paul's open. Then he saw the leakage. The bandage under her arm came off, and he could see the blood. He could see the hole. She wasn't aware of the bleeding or that the dressing had loosened. He didn't want to continue, but dutifully Paul kept on. In the middle of this outrageous scenario, they heard a car pull into the driveway. It beeped. It was Bobby Ray and a hooker. Paul was relieved, having an excuse to decouple, and he rushed into the bathroom to wash up quickly. That's when Kathy saw the blood. She never said a word, just gathered up the sheets and put them in the hamper. She never said a word, until now as her spirit washed over Paul with acknowledgment.

The visit with Bobby Ray was mercifully brief, just a drunken how-dee-do, as Paul was only wearing pants and Kathy had on a bathrobe and a swami towel on her head. It was evident that the Cleaver's weren't receiving today. When Bobby Ray and Bubbles left, Paul was purposely nonchalant. Kathy, in a hushed voice, said, "Paul, I was raped once."

For once, Paul didn't overreact. He was measured. Pissed, but measured.

"When, what happened, did they catch the guy?" asked Paul.

"It wasn't like that," she said slowly. "I was at a smoker, and I got pretty drunk, and I don't remember anything really, except that I woke up in this Potter's apartment, in bed, and I was very sore." She came over and sat next to Paul on the sofa. "I knew I was molested, didn't know how many guys or how many times or anything. I also knew that it was going to be my word against theirs, so to follow up would be fruitless." Paul knew that the Potters were the jock fraternity on SUNY's Albany campus. He wasn't angry, but he felt terrible for Kathy's apparent angst. It seemed to Paul that she felt somehow responsible for the rape. He held her close and said, "I'm sorry that it happened, but it doesn't make a difference to me. It just makes me feel bad for you, and I wish I could take the pain away." He meant it. Paul wasn't a self-centered prick all the time. She said, "I love you so much." Paul caressed a little girl, like a daddy would, to make things better. And it really did.

As she slept in his arms, he recalled, sex in the sixties wasn't quite what it was cracked up to be. He remembered his first time. This was the memory that he never shared with anyone. It was so embarrassing. He had plenty of opportunities to discard his virginity in high school. The girls seemed to like him, and there were plenty of loose women around the projects. But he always stopped before going "all the way." Probably some foolish Catholic voodoo fear. But when he was in jump school and figured he was going to Viet Nam to die, he decided he didn't want to die a virgin. He also knew that he wasn't going to meet a nice girl being a soldier. Nice girls in army towns ran like mice away from any G.I. Even more so one from New York.

Paul decided that the best bet was to go to a whorehouse. It was too easy to find a whorehouse, courtesy of Uncle Sam. All a trooper had to do was to go to the bulletin board in the company square and look at the list of places that were "off-limits." It was like yellow pages for sex, drugs, and rock 'n' roll. He found the name of the Dixie Hotel, and he liked the sound of that, almost prophetic. It was one last task to perform before his passage into war, just in case he got his balls shot off.

Get advice from a seasoned pro. Paul was a good planner.

He looked up PFC Kronovich. Kronovich was a bitter twenty-six-year-old who had gotten divorced. Unfortunately for PFC Kronovich, as his marriage dissolved, so did his selective service deferment. Kronovich thought he was safe from the draft, but he wasn't. At twenty-six, he was almost at the upper age limit for call-up. Two weeks to go to age twenty-seven. His ex called the local draft board. Then, she called Kronovich. Ergo, the bitterness. He was Paul's adviser in all things adult with the now unspoken exception of draft deferments. Paul told him his plans for the evening and got his marching orders. This was gospel. "Okay, make sure you drink a lot before you go," the teacher started. "You'll last a lot longer that way. You want to make sure that you get your money's worth. Also, make sure you jerk off before you get there because it's your first time and you'll probably come too quick." Paul appreciated the advice and got his khakis on, bloused boots, paratrooper wings, glider patch and, most importantly, clean boxers with nary a hole in them. He was mission ready.

Paul caught the bus downtown. When he got to the bus station, he knew there were peep shows in the lobby. It was kind of like a nickelodeon thing where you put a dime in this machine and hand-cranked the wheel and pictures fell one after the other to create the effect of movement. It was a black and white strip show, gal about forty, big hooters, big smile. She got naked after twenty cents' worth. Paul was bonered up, walked into the men's room, paid a nickel, got a stall, and beat the bishop. He cleaned himself up as best he could. Then, he went into the first joint with booze. He drank about five beers and ran into a couple of "legs." Legs were guys who were regular soldiers, not paratroopers. They were on weekend pass from basic training, and, because Paul was airborne, they looked up to him even though he was a good two years younger.

They bought him a lot more brew and a couple of shots. Eventually, Paul announced, "I'm gonna get laid. If you guys want to rent some pussy, follow me." Spoken like a true leader, though he couldn't imagine MacArthur saying quite the same inspirational words. Follow him they did, right down to the Dixie Hotel. The building was a five-story brick and wood deal, old, probably fulfilling its final destiny here.

Paul marched into the lobby, his two-man squad directly behind him, in awe of him at this juncture. "Hey, you got girls?" demanded Paul to a well-dressed, dark-skinned man behind the desk.

The man didn't even look up when he methodically recited his litany. "You got to rent a room for the night, $12 each. You got to rent a washcloth and towel, $1 each. When you get to the room you just rented, there will be a young lady there to welcome you. Any further negotiations are up to you and the young lady. Questions?"

"Nope," said the leader and wished his troopers good luck. He paid the man $14. As did his followers.

Paul got the key to room 335 and asked for the elevator, eliciting a chuckle from the well- dressed man. "There's your elevator," said the man, pointing to the staircase while handing him a white towel and washcloth. Paul went up to the room, never once thinking that the reason that this place could be off-limits was because they mugged G.I.'s. He opened 335 with the key, which was attached to a huge green paddle serving as a key ring. On his entrance to a well-lit room, he saw a pretty blonde, about twenty-five years old, sitting on the bed. To Paul, it looked as if she had been crying.

Truth was, she had just swallowed two nasal inhalers for a speed buzz. Paul's first words were, "Have you been crying? Is everything okay?" Quite a question. Is everything okay? Because here you are, a pretty blonde, in a shit hotel, in a shit army town, at nine o'clock at night, trading your body with strangers for money? Sure, things are just ducky, couldn't be better. How's the family?

"I'm fine, honey. What kind of a date y'all looking for," she asked.

"Ah, what," responded Paul.

"What kind of date y'all want, honey? Half 'n' half, straight fuck, blow job?" indexed the professional.

Paul said, "Jeez, I don't know. Straight fuck, I guess. This is my first time, and I'm going to Viet Nam, and I don't want to get my dick shot off or get killed and never know what it's like to fuck."

She laughed, "Yeah, I hear that a lot. How much money you got, sweetheart?"

Paul reached into his khakis and came up with a twenty. "I've got twenty dollars, but I need thirty-five cents to get the bus back to the fort tomorrow."

Being the consummate businesswoman that she was, she offered, "Here's thirty-five cents for the bus, give me the twenty." Deal. "Okay, get undressed, honey." Paul sat on the bed and started to remove his boots. He couldn't get the knot out of the bootlace in the second boot. She looked at him impatiently, and he figured she thought he was stalling. He ripped his boot off from the back. That took a great deal of strength, but it was necessary. He just had his hole-less boxers on when he stood in front of his evening's rental. She looked at his Johnson and said, with amazement, "Honey, there's toilet paper all over your dick!"

Paul flushed, "Oh well, umm, I caught my dick in my zipper, and it was bleeding. It's okay now, though."

She laughed, "Jerked off, didn't ya? That's okay, everybody does." She cleaned him off, making him instantly hard, and precisely one minute and twelves seconds later, Paul was a man.

The woman left soon after, and Paul fell asleep. At ten o'clock the following morning, there was a loud knock on the door. "Okay, Romeo, time to check out," said the unseen voice. Paul rose, got dressed, and couldn't figure out what had happened to his jump boot which was ripped. He sure couldn't blouse them, so he pulled his khaki pants over the top of the boot, now worrying that he would be out of uniform, with his jump wings on his chest and his glider patch on his overseas cap. When he got outside, he had little trouble orienting himself to the bus depot but had a good deal of trouble walking with the flapping boot.

On the bus, he felt remorse. *What if I get killed,* thought Paul. *This is, without a doubt, a mortal sin.* Not only fucking but paying to fuck. *I'm screwed,* thought Paul. Screwed for being screwed. Screwy. When he got off the bus, he jumped into an on-post shuttle and went directly to his barracks for a shower and some beef jerky he kept hidden in his locker. When he got there, one of the guys said, "Hey, Fogarty, you just getting in?" Paul said, "Yeah, went downtown and got laid last night."

Paul was not impressed with this whole fucking business. For all the fanfare, he expected more. To him, it seemed like, "Okay, that was super, now what?" Not that he ever stopped, though he did go a whole year once without fucking, just to see if he could do it. And once he screwed four different women in one twenty-four-hour period. He was always doing self-discipline shit like that. No real reason, probably some weird kind of OCD, he figured.

Now, his mind and body returned to the cemetery. He was sweating now, having turned the heater on full blast. Finally, he turned the ignition off and got out of the car. He walked over to her grave, stood at the foot of the plot, and said, softly, "Fuck the Potters."

Chapter 18

"My dog only shits on Polack's graves."

In the distance, an old guy with one of those puffy thermal jackets was walking his dog. His dog was sniffing around, jumping from grave to grave, marking his territory with urine on some of them. The man got close to Paul and waved. Paul waved back, and, as feared, the guy came up to talk.

"How ya' doin' buddy?" asked the old-timer.

"Okay," said Paul, just knowing this guy wanted to be his new best friend.

Curmudgeon said, "I walk my dog here, every single day. And you know what? He'll pee on any grave, but he'll only shit on Polack graves. Crazy, huh?"

Paul nodded, acknowledging this extremely doubtful piece of information.

"It's like he can read, for Chrissake! Soon as he gets near a ski clubber, bingo, bowels open. And he really squats and strains. Never the same one either. Hope he doesn't run out of Polacks or he'll be bound up sure as shit."

Enthralled as he was at this novel phenomenon, Paul just kind of snickered and hoped the man and his apparently Nazi canine would continue their search for a new target to bowel bombard. No such luck. This guy was a talker.

"My wife's buried up on the hill. I come to see her every day. She died twelve years ago, had the cancer. She died rough but never complained. Tried to cook and clean like she wasn't sick, but she got tired and weak. Don't figure I was much help but had to work to keep the insurance, you know."

Paul had never heard so much talk about medical insurance until he got up in this part of New York State. It seemed to be a big deal for these folks. The old guy continued, "I worked at the paper mill, most everybody did. Most of us guys came back from the big one and went to work at the plant. Good job, good pay, and benefits. But around '75, the government decided we were putting too much shit into the river. The company decided to move to the south where the tree huggers weren't so powerful, like up here. Got a fair-sized buy-out from the company though, invested the dough into a trophy shop. I make plaques and trophies, shit like that. I still do it out of my house, if you ever need something like that. I even made a wall plaque for my late wife and glued it onto the headstone, but the prick caretaker, who I believe is a fag, took it off. Ain't seen you here before. Who ya visiting?"

Paul was kind of taken with this lonely, old, pejorative laced plaque-maker.

"An old girlfriend. Took me a while to get up here. First time, actually."

"Want to know why you're really up here? I'll tell you why. 'Cause you figure you're gonna die pretty soon. Seen it before. You're making peace with your own self, ain't ya?"

God damn! Was it that obvious? Who the hell was this guy? And how could he possibly know?

The guy said, "Kathryn, huh. That's her name. Urbanski?"

Paul said, "Yeah, and don't let your Polack-hating dog shit on this grave, okay? She's a mick."

Old-timer promised, "You got my word, buddy, I'm a mick my own self."

Paul was bemused but thankful. The dog was probably thinking, *Yeah, but it's okay for you Irish pricks to run over dogs in the middle of the street.* Or maybe not.

The old-timer then started to walk away. He was kind of bent over and had no gloves on his hands, though he was wearing a Russian-type gulag hat.

Paul called after him, "Hey, what's your name?"

Old Guy called back, "Peter Murphy."

Funny, thought Paul, *last guy on earth I talk to before going to see Saint Peter is a guy named Peter.* Paul said, "Take these gloves, will ya? I've got about ten pairs of these, and I can see you got big hands like me."

The old guy took the gloves and said, "Thanks, didn't catch your name."

"Paul, Paul Fogarty," said Paul. The man surprised Paul when he asked, "Why are you giving me these gloves, really? Your big hands get as cold as mine." Paul then reached into his pocket and tried to hand over a bunch of folded over money. He couldn't talk, but he looked directly into the eyes of the stranger, who was no longer a stranger but more of a fellow traveler. The man looked at him, then took the money but didn't put it into his pocket, just stared back at Paul. He said, holding his gaze steady, "Don't do it, Paul Fogarty. You have no right. No fucking right at all."

Paul turned his back on the old man and just raised his left hand in a "stay out of my business gesture." Peter stood there for a few minutes and said once more, "You don't have the right." He then called out to his dog, and he and the prejudiced mutt went out the main gate. Paul went back to the grave and tried to think about where he was mentally before the interruption. It took a few minutes of reflection, and he tried to picture Kathy's smile. Man, that girl could smile. Her teeth were just flawed enough to make them uniquely attractive. Her whole face congealed into one big happy mask when she was pleased. Which was often, and for little things as well as big. The serious side of her suited her personality characteristics perfectly, though Paul didn't really like to see them coming. He liked it better when she was happy. Before she ever told him anything of import, she put the "I'm serious" face on. And she always looked him in the eye when she relayed the skinny. He guessed that she was instantly processing his reactions. She was that smart.

One time when they were living together, she put the serious flag up and said, "Paul, I want to tell you something. Hear me out, please. I don't want to do anything behind your back, but I'm very serious about this."

Paul looked back at her. "Sure, babe, what's up?"

Kathy said, "A lot of the teachers and students are going down to DC to participate in the moratorium against the war. I've thought it over, and I've decided to go. I hope you are not angry with me. I know how you feel about the war. It's something I have to do."

Paul was surprised. He wasn't surprised that she was going to this thing, but rather that she thought he would take offense or see it as disloyalty. He told her, "Thanks for telling me, but I respect your right to protest that war. And what in Christ's name made you think that I was a proponent of that war? My friends are getting fucked up every day for shit. I just don't see what good going down there is gonna do. The politicians don't give a shit. They just want to make money for the war business guys, who will keep them in power. You guys are pissing into the wind."

She considered this. "Maybe so, but we've got to try. Would you consider going?"

Paul said, "No, I can't. I think most of the guys that are going to march are just too fucking scared to get drafted and get stuck in that place."

She replied, "Okay, just so you know, I love you with every fiber of my being." Where did she come up with stuff like that? Every fiber of my being? Damn, that was downright poetic.

"Yeah me too. Don't ever doubt that, Kath."

"I don't," she said, grabbing at this straw from Paul.

In retrospect, Paul thought, *how many people were under the misconception that because a guy went to war, he was pro-war?* Kathy was the smartest person he had ever met, and obviously, she thought so. These were mostly just poor kids who got drafted or lied to by a recruiter and tried to get it over with. The most thoughts politic these guys had was, I'll vote for any broad with big tits. Even when they came back, most guys didn't give a shit one way or the other about the war. If they made it home in one piece, or if they made it home at all, they were more than satisfied that their political views concerning this war were of absolutely no relevance to their present circumstances. Were they changed? Yes. Were their views changed? In most cases, they really didn't have a political opinion, and there was certainly no reason for them to have one now. People would ask them, "What do you think of the war? You were there." What were you supposed to say? "Well, I spent a year over there and didn't really give a fuck why we were there or what the outcome for world peace was going to be?" Instead, you said, "Well, it's complicated." End of political viewpoint. Period.

The wind whipped up a little, in spurts. Paul stuck his big hands into his leather jacket. He guessed that now was as good a time as any. Before retrieving the shotgun, Paul got down on his knees at the foot of the grave. He said his trilogy of prayers aloud. Then he looked at the dirt. "I'm gonna do this fast, Kathy, 'cause I'm a little nervous. I hope that you know how much I love you and how much I want to see you again."

Previously, Paul had considered leaving a note. But the fact that his headless body would be lying on this grave, brains leaking out, shotgun discharged, shouldn't pose too much of a problem for the detectives working on the case. A note wouldn't be necessary. *Melodramatic bullshit, anyway.* The act, the deed—that was his suicide note. And the only written material that would matter would be the last will and testament that he left in the big green safe at home. His ex knew where it was and would make sure his wishes were honored. She would never understand why he did this, nor would his kids, with maybe the exception of his oldest son. Though Paul had never discussed this woman of his past with his son, or the way he felt about her, he always thought that his son sensed something about his dad. Something sad in his eyes. Moments of reflection that his son had observed in his unaware father deeply involved. Paul kind of hoped that they would get on with their lives as soon as possible and have mostly happy memories of him. He was, at least, a good provider, if not a good example. And they would have plenty of dough.

Another piece of his last will and testament was that his mortal remains were to be buried in the Solomon National Cemetery at Saratoga Springs, New York. This was a veterans' cemetery that was not that old. It was a beautiful place, not like the frozen tundra he was standing on here. He had visited the place many times and had laid to rest more than a few of his buddies there. What he liked about it the most was that you were buried in the order that you died. No favoritism, officer or enlisted, war hero or supply clerk. Eminently and finally fair, just and righteous. Paul recalled his buddy, PFC Patrick O'Shaughnessy, USMC, Viet Nam, who drank himself to death, ironically being buried next to James Holt-Smyth, USN, WWII, a judge in civilian life who had sentenced Patrick to thirty-day stints in the county jail repeatedly. Now they were eternal bunkmates. Cool. Plus, the guys kept the cemetery spotless and trimmed. No tipped over headstones in Saratoga. Neat as a pin. Paul always liked neat.

It was time. Paul got up off his knees and headed for the trunk of the car. *Where the fuck were those keys?* Oh yeah, in the ignition. Paul was remarkably clear-headed. It was like he was moving as an actor in a film at this point, knowing that he just had to keep on keepin' on. As he opened the driver door, he reached in for the keys. No keys. *Here we go again.* He looked all around the front seat, on the ground, in his pockets and finally in the trunk lock. Nowhere to be found. *What the hell?* Then, he noticed a small card stuck under the windshield wiper. *What the fuck?* He took it, put his glasses on, and read the business card.

Peter Murphy
Plaque, Medallion, and Trophy Shop
P.O. Box 1531,
Cattaraugus, NY 14719
Telephone 716-543-9133

The wind whipped up a little, blowing off a decaying piece of dog shit from near Kathy's grave.

Chapter 19

A Bait Store Stinks Too Much

"Son of a bitch!" Paul yelled. *That old bastard took my goddamned keys.* Paul tried kicking the trunk open with no luck. He grabbed a piece of a tree limb that was lying there and tried to pry it open. Again, no cigar. Paul still had his cell phone with him and dialed the number on the card. He got the answering machine. Before the poorly taped message completed, he yelled, "Pick the goddamned phone up, Murphy. Pick it up now!" He heard a click on the other end.

"Hello, that you, Paul? Figured you'd be giving me a call."

"You got my car keys, you son of a bitch?"

"Yup. Didn't figure you'd be needing them."

Paul said, "What made you think you could take my keys? What gives you the right?"

Murphy laughed, "Don't talk to me about rights. What I did was nothing compared to what you're going to do."

Paul took up the challenge in Murphy's voice. "And what makes you think you have any idea of what I'm going to do, you old fuck?" The answer took Paul by surprise. Murphy said, "It's *because* I'm an old fuck that I know what you're going to do. You're going to end it all. And right there, on that spot that I left you. And you don't have the right. I figured you were going to need your car for something, so I took the keys and left my card. You owe me the right to get a reason for all this. I was there for a reason, you idiot. You owe yourself an explanation, at least one last time."

Paul was pissed but intrigued. "Get your wrinkled old ass up here right now and give me those keys."

Murphy said, "Or what? You'll kick my ass? You don't even know where I am, and you gave me all your money, so you're not going anywhere. I'll pick you up but won't tell you where I've hidden the car keys until you and me have a coffee or a beer and talk about this shit. If you can convince me, I'll give you the keys." Checkmate. Paul agreed to this bizarre proposal. Who the hell was this guy? What was going on here? If Paul had tried to explain this turn of events to someone or to try and write it down, it would seem so unlikely as to be unreal.

Paul sat in his car. He sat there for an hour, no Murphy. His fucking hands were cold. Where was this guy? It was all part of Murphy's newly hatched plan. Let him stew for a little.

Murphy had been around, knew the score. He wasn't always a dog-walking chatterbox. The old-timer was a smart guy and a hell of a soldier, back in the big one, double-u-double-u-deuce. He had seen death in many ways, and he knew the value of life. It wasn't a choice for Murphy, wasn't anyone's right to take any life, especially not one's own. When the unit that Murphy served in liberated the Dachau concentration camp, in April '45, Murphy was one of the first to enter. He saw the walking skeletons, saw the crematorium and piles of cordwood corpses in the boxcars, naked, covered only partially by some freshly fallen snow. And freakishly, he saw the sundogs on that day, guiding him to the crematorium.

Peter Murphy remembered that his Battalion Commander was so irate at what he was witnessing on the entrance to the camp, that he let the inmates deliver their own form of justice to what remained of the camp's SS cadre. He just had his guys pull out of the camp for a half-hour, supposedly setting up a defensive perimeter and then re-entered. There were twenty or thirty fresh bodies, well-fed, some blond-headed, some in inmate uniforms trying to pass themselves off as victims. They were now the victims, paying with their lives in the ferocity of those surviving camp inmates strong enough and vengeful enough to savagely beat these jailers to their deaths. Murphy remembered hundreds of living corpses wandering down the wide barrack streets. Dazed, confused, and fearful, they had every expression but happiness. They were humans who were unable to smile or cry or emote in any way. Their systematic torture proved so successful that these survivors appeared devoid of any feelings, physical or psychological. The only thing that Murphy did feel was that these people somehow had retained their dignity, despite their naked, shuffling gait. Despite their fantastic belief that freedom was now upon them, they walked as one massive consciousness. A supreme valedictory processional.

The old man had seen a lot of horrifying things during that war. This was the capstone. The watershed event of his life, where he learned the value of life and the right to live it to the end. An end not of your own making, but of the eternal energy that commands the same.

Peter Murphy pulled his red, apparently held together only by rust, pick-up truck through the main gate of the graveyard and pulled up to where Paul was standing. Without a trace of embarrassment or repentance, he just said, "Hop in." As if he were picking up a guy to go to work or something. Paul just shook his head and entered the truck on the passenger side. He slammed the door shut, and it didn't feel like it was secured because of the rust, but somehow it was. Instinctively, he reached for the seat belt, which, of course, was non-existent.

"See what I mean," said Murphy. "If you really wanted to die, you wouldn't be reaching for a seat belt."

Paul laughed, "It's just a habit, old man."

"So's living."

Fortunately, the diarrheic dog was not on board. Unfortunately, the window on Paul's side wouldn't shut, so despite the heater being on full blast, Paul's scrotum was entering the abdominal sanctuary.

"Where're my keys?" asked Paul.

"All in good time, my friend, all in good time," answered Peter.

Frozen motor oil and grease has a unique smell, thought Paul, as this truck was a mobile shrine to both. It reminded him of the way the trucks used to smell in West Germany during maneuvers. Murphy had also grown used to this feel and smell since the passage through France and Germany during the war. This was part of an unconscious communion between these two men. They rode through the village in silence, Paul thinking, *I'm supposed to already be dead.* After about four miles out came to a left turn. Paul couldn't tell if it was a paved or dirt road, but it was narrow. They wound their way through blown snow and some bare patches, finally landing at a small bungalow with some seriously heavy smoke coming from two chimneys. The mine-laying dog came barking up to the truck, guiding it into the tracks that served as the driveway. "C'mon in. Let's get warmed up, get us a cup of joe." Paul was beyond words at this point and just fell into line walking into the house, having to duck his head under the poor excuse for wind chimes hanging off the lentil.

The house was warm, almost cozy. Furniture was plentiful, albeit cheap, covered with inexpensive slipcovers. The kind that Paul had grown up with. *You can cover a lot of sins with slipcovers,* thought Paul. The couch was long and low. Paul took a seat as Peter lit up a cigarette.

"I'm going to make us some coffee. Not that shit Instamatic stuff either. I percolate mine. Tastes goddamned good too. Never let it perk less than three or more than five."

Paul inquired, "Less than three or more than five what?"

Murphy raised his eyebrows. "Why, minutes, you goddamned fool. Whaddya think I meant?" He rustled about in the small kitchen that had a gas and gas stove—Paul hadn't seen one of these babies in thirty-five years. He set up the ancient percolator, adjusted the flame, and said to Paul,

"C'mon over to the garage, I'll show you my workshop. Where I make my plaques and stuff."

Paul said, "Where're my fucking keys, Murphy?"

Murphy said with a smile, "We're getting there. Relax. What's your hurry? You got something to do, somewhere to go?"

They had to go back out the front door and into another, recessed door about ten feet away that Paul hadn't even noticed. It wasn't shoveled, but the footsteps patterns were mosaics out in the ice and snow. Now, Paul saw where at least one of the smoke sources was coming from. It was downright hot in this room that was serving as a workshop, but it was remarkably neat and tidy. Plaques, medallions, and, indeed, trophies were standing on several sets of cheap veneer shelving or hanging on the wall. They were put there as models or displays when Murphy was showing for a sale. Truth be told, they were all orders that either hadn't been picked up or hadn't been paid for. Murphy was a practical man, not wasteful at all.

The tour guide started pointing out his laboratory. "This here's my drill press, here's my saw, router and this is my workbench. Where I do most of my stuff. I've seen those plaques and stuff done by some damned computer. Garbage. Takes away the human touch. All the shit comes out looking the same. No art to it, see. No fucking originality. I hate that computer shit."

Paul bit. "How long you been doing this?"

"I've been at it since my payout from the paper company. I was gonna open a bait shop, 'cause I like to fish, but a bait store stinks too much. At least, according to my wife it does," said Murphy.

Paul couldn't believe he was having this conversation.

"How did you learn how to do it?"

Peter swelled with pride at this one. "Believe it or not, I took a correspondence course. You know, lessons that came in the mail. Only cost me $74, plus tax. But I deducted it from my taxes, and I can deduct all my materials and labor from the taxes too. Know where I found out about the correspondence course? This is the best part. On a fucking matchbook cover. Yup, that's right. I was thinking about what to do, lit up a Lucky, and saw it on the matches. Never regretted it either. Sometimes God gives you a message that doesn't include a fucking lightning bolt, ya' know."

Paul knew. Murphy put another log in the fireplace and said to Paul, "I've got glue drying on a couple of plaques, nothing like wood heat to cure them." He then turned out the lights, and they left to go back to the main house, *for what only God knows,* thought Paul.

The smell of the freshly perked coffee was welcoming them, and Paul wondered whether the more than three, less than five rule was observed. He suspected it was. This old guy was set in his ways, but he seemed to have his shit together. Paul again sat on the couch and saw a small television set with, unbelievably, rabbit ears. There was no doubt that it was a black and white model. *This friggen joint could be a museum,* thought Paul.

Murphy came in with two steaming mugs of freshly percolated coffee. "Hope you don't need no sugar or milk. I don't put none of that pussy shit in my coffee. Wasn't meant to be drunk that way. I like it black and strong," opined the waiter.

"Smells good," said Paul. *And it does smell good,* Paul thought. Maybe the old guy had something here with his damned percolator. They both sat and sipped their black, perked coffee. It was a couple of guys who could have been old chums, instead of the reality of these bizarre circumstances.

"Coffee's good, Peter," said Paul. "What the hell is going on here? What the hell are you trying to do?"

"Well," said Murphy, "I'm not trying to save your life, Paul. I'm just trying to give you a different viewpoint. You know, it's a funny thing. I really do walk my dog every day in the cemetery. Thing is, I do it at just about the same time every day. About seven in the morning, never later than eight. But for some reason today, I was messing around and doing stuff I never do. My damned dog, Barney's his name, by the way, kept on looking at me like I was nuts. So, I took him over to the graveyard, figuring his guts was about to come out. Soon as I saw you, I knew you were in trouble. Something drew me over to you, like a goddamned magnet or something. I could see it in your face, your eyes."

Murphy took a sip. "Ahhh, coffee is one of God's wonders. When I was in the war, sometimes guys would look at me, and I just knew that they were gonna be dead pretty soon. I think they knew it too. Fact is, I know they did. You had the same goddamned look, Paul. The exact same look. I knew what it was. I wish I didn't, but I did."

Paul took this in, and surprisingly had no trouble whatsoever believing every word the old man said. "Okay," Paul said, "well, if that's the case, so be it. What gave you the right to steal my keys, to interfere with my decision. Who the fuck are you?"

Murphy lit up a Lucky. "I'll tell you who the fuck I am, Paul. I'm the guy who is supposed to die before you do. I'm the guy who knows what life is. Do you think for one second that I don't want to join my wife? Who I miss? Every day seems like a year. But I don't have the right. And you don't either. If you did, God wouldn't have put me in that graveyard, at that time, to steal your goddamned keys. And if you don't believe in God, well maybe it was your girlfriend put me there, and my late wife put me there.

"Maybe they're chums in the great beyond. Who the fuck cares? Don't matter, I was there, got your keys, got your ass, and here you are. Now you are going to have to hear me out. Most important, you are going to have to think about what you intended to do. And to think about the real problems, not what gave me the right to take your keys, but what gives you the right to take time from God. Or whatever the fuck you believe in."

Murphy looked Paul dead in the eye with this diatribe. "So, I'm going to ask you nice, please listen to me and talk to me. Maybe you and I can figure this shit out. I know you think you should be dead right now. I've got no doubt you're serious. But you're here, so give me some time. Hell, maybe you and I will do the Dutch act together. Maybe you'll convince me. I promise that I'll listen to you, not just hear you. All I ask is that you listen to me and give it a chance. Fair enough?"

Peter and Paul drained their cups.

It was on.

Chapter 20

Peanut Butter on Devil's Food Cake

"Let me tell you a little story, Paul," said Murphy. "It'll show you how good intentions can get a little fucked up. When I was a kid, we lived down there in the village. It was a neighborhood where everybody knew everybody. And we respected our elders. Had to, or you'd get the shit kicked out of you quick. Anyways, there was this old-timer, used to sit outside in spring, summer, and fall. He was a Spanish war vet, and he lived by himself. I used to help him with his coal and garbage and stuff, and he'd give me a few cents. Mostly though, I loved talking to him because he was always teaching me stuff. Like how to milk a grasshopper, or how to tell what time it was by just looking at the sun. His name was Sheehy, and he was fond of a pint or two when he could afford it."

Paul put his feet up on a slipcovered ottoman, listening. Murphy continued. "Anyways, it was my birthday, and my mother asked me what kind of a cake I wanted. I could have whatever I wanted. I asked her for a devil's food cake, with peanut butter frosting. Now, today I know that seems kind of disgusting, but in my eyes, this was the best of all confectionary combinations that could ever be constructed. She rolled her eyes but said she'd do it. And she did. The cake was delicious, even though no one else took more than a sliver after I blew out the candles and made my wish. Okay with me, more for me. Next day I take a good size piece over to my good friend Mr. Sheehy. I told him this was my birthday cake, and this was his piece. He smiled his toothless smile and said, 'Well, thank you, Pistol Pete.' He used to call me Pistol Pete. He took a couple of good size bites, kind of made a funny face, eyes started bugging out, and down he goes. He was blue, Paul. I didn't know what to do. I kept yelling his name, and then he just stopped moving. His mouth was open, but it was full of cake, and I just ran over to my house and got my mom and told her what happened. She ran over with me and told me to go down and get the dentist, who was a few houses away. I did, and over we came.

"Mr. Sheehy was dead. Choked to death, they said. I just cried and cried. It was my first brush with death, and I didn't like it. Also, it was my fault. The dentist—Mr. Gold was his name, can't make that up—asked me what in God's green earth I was thinking by giving an old toothless guy peanut butter cake. And with nothing to drink."

Murphy's eyes looked like they were tearing up a little. Might just be cataracts, though, thought Paul. He went on, "I was an altar boy, so I had to serve at the funeral. There was only two of us in town, and Billy had a broken leg. I was convinced that all the people attending the service, there were about ten people there, knew that I was the boy who killed Mr. Sheehy. About halfway through the services, the candle I was holding blew out. This was, to me, a sure sign from God that I was responsible for the old timer's death. The priest didn't bat an eye and re-lit the candle, which stayed lit for the rest of the funeral."

Paul was transfixed as the story continued, and he assured him, "He probably had a heart attack, Murphy. What makes you think you killed him? Sure sounds like a heart attack to me."

Murphy said, "You're not the first person to say that, Paul. It's a nice thing to say, but old man Sheehy was doing just fine until I gave him the peanut butter cake. Nope, I killed him all right. Didn't mean to, but surer than shit, I killed him." Murphy got up and went to the kitchen. "Want another coffee? We ain't going to sleep for a while."

Paul thought that was a pretty presumptuous statement. "Nope, none for me." Murphy got himself a cup. Drank it cold, too. He went on, "You're probably wondering why I told you that story. The reason is that I really liked that old guy. And the only reason I shared my cake with him is because he was my friend and I was proud of 'inventing' the recipe, I guess. I lived with the memory of his face just staring at me when he couldn't breathe and how helpless I felt. The fact is, I know now that even though I was not the instrument of his death, I was certainly incidental in it. But it was his time. He didn't kill himself. I don't think he wanted to die, but he did, and now I know that it's okay. It was just his time. Like mine's coming soon, I guess."

Paul said, "That's a nice story, but what the hell does that have to do with me?"

Peter Murphy was ready with the answer. "I was getting to that. Hold your horses. I went to Sheehy's house, gave him the cake, and he died. I went to his house almost every day. I also go to the cemetery every day. I met you. You are still alive. Sheehy would have lived a little or a lot longer, had I not gone to his house that day. That was my part in his death. You have lived a little or maybe a lot longer because I went to the cemetery at that time. That's my part in your life. It all equals out. Make sense?"

Paul hated to admit it, but it did make a strange kind of karma-like sense. He said, "Well, Murphy, if that's all you got to say then I appreciate it, now give me my keys. You did your best."

Murphy said, "Not by a longshot, Paul. Not by a fucking longshot. You want to know why I was coming in your direction at the graveyard? Because buried right next to your girlfriend is John Sheehy. You want to add that to the list of 'coincidences?' You want to believe that God or somebody or something is asking you to reconsider? Grieve, yes, but live your life until your time. Fogarty, you don't have the right."

Paul was shocked. *Wow,* if this was true, then indeed, something spiritual or spooky was going on. He tried to wrap his head around this latest bit of information. His chest suddenly started itching, and he reached into his coat to scratch. He immediately felt something stiff in his pocket. When he looked down, he saw the library signature card, K. Shanahan. Man, oh man, he leaned back into the sofa and covered his eyes with his forearm. Paul thought out loud, "What in the hell is going on here?"

Murphy asked, "Want a shot of scotch, Paul?"

Paul toyed with the idea but then said, "Don't drink."

Murphy smiled. "Didn't figure you did Paul. Didn't figure you did. You're way past that test, ain't ya? I'm going to shut the lights off and go to bed. You close your eyes and think about what's going on here. I'm going to get you a nice warm quilt my wife made." Funny thing was, this was exactly what Paul wanted to do.

The older man then said, "Paul, your keys are on the coffee table. I hope you don't take them, but if you do, I'll drive you back to the cemetery and your car whenever you want. Get some shuteye. See you in the morning."

Chapter 21

"Never had no kids, till now."

Murphy went off to bed. Paul lay on the sofa, pulling his mothball-smelling quilt up to his waist. His mind was jumbled from the turn of events that this day had taken. He couldn't help but think that he was supposed to be dead right now. *Maybe I'm dead,* thought Paul. Maybe he had already pulled the trigger, and all of this was some form of life recollection with a heavenly aide named Murphy guiding him through his thoughts. No, that was absurd. Paul finally concluded, *whatever happened, happened.* Whatever was going to happen, had to happen. The keys were in front of his eyes. He was back in control. Or was he? He would be forced to recollect.

Paul shut the table lamp off, overwhelmingly exhausted. Mentally he was sharp, but physically, his body screamed for sleep. The only light and sounds came from the fireplace. It was the perfect sanctorum for reflection. Paul's mind super-scanned not only today's events, but many others also. It seemed to him his childhood, military, and adult experiences washed over his brain like a tsunami. He focused on a park, down by the projects, where he used to go when he was a kid. There were four baseball fields in a square mile area in North Albany. There was a priest, named Father Fearus. *Again, can't make this stuff up,* thought Paul, who believed that the male child "cliff dwellers"—the bottomland house living locals derisive name for the project's inhabitants—would all be saved by just playing baseball. Football and basketball were acceptable substitutes, but apparently, Jesus preferred baseball. Father Fearus was famous for two things: handing out baseball gloves, balls, and bats to every projects male he could get his mitts on, *pun intended*, and blessing the apartments in the projects, giving out a picture of the Ted Nugent look-alike Jesus to all. This was no easy task, the blessings. Every time a "family" had a new baby, they were upgraded to a bigger apartment in the gulag. Every time a kid got drafted or killed or ran away or went to jail, the Albany Housing Authority downgraded them to a smaller domicile. With three hundred units in the projects, Father Fearus sprinkled a lot of holy water, but if the clients weren't newbies, they had to hand-carry their Jesus Christ superstar picture to the new destination, where it got re-blessed.

The central park, by PS #20, was Paul's favorite. There was a fifty-foot tall tree overlooking the field and school. It was an easy climb. Paul would climb the tree all hours of the day and night. He would go right to the top, never afraid. There was a fork in the crest that Paul could rest his skinny fanny on, and he would pretend he was in the crow's nest of a pirate ship or a bird flying when the wind blew. Even in the winter, Paul would climb, but it wasn't as good because there were no leaves to hide him from people staring. Right now, on this sofa, Paul's mind transported him to that tree, on top, at peace with the world. "I'm the king of the pirates, the beast of the seas. All who see me will regret the day they were born."

Paul, the king of the pirates, beast of the seas, fell into a deep sleep. The demons didn't wait long. The demons wanted him this night.

Nightmare number one was a regular. Paul was naked, firing his rifle at the barbed wire. He couldn't see the enemy. All he could hear the cries and screams of the wounded, on both sides, and he was running out of ammo. The RPG was coming right at him, slow motion, but he couldn't get away.

He woke with a gasp. It took him a couple of minutes to acclimate to his new surroundings. Murphy's fireplace was the key to his recall.

Standard fare for Paul, he went back to sleep.

Number two was a frigid night in the projects. He was about twelve years old. It was 3:30 in the morning, and he was, again, locked out of his apartment, his mother's way of punishing him for real and imagined transgressions. It was well below freezing, and the boiler room that was usually his refuge was mysteriously locked. Paul was fucked. This nightmare was really a memory, no distortion at all. It was scarier than number one because it happened—more than once, actually. There was no waking up from this one.

Somehow the interminable cold just lasted and hurt. The quiet concrete and cold blacktop. One was so alone. It was about seven miles to the bowling alley up on Broadway. Open twenty-four hours. If they didn't throw him out, he would be okay. It was a long walk up, and *it'll be a long walk back in the morning,* but he had to do something. So, he'd start walking toward the bowling alley. "Man, I'm hungry," thought Paul, talking in his sleep. That's when he woke up. He was so grateful to be warm that he cried to himself. Paul thought, *Is this a nightmare or a memory?* Didn't much matter, it just never stopped coming. Even though that misery was finally over, the dream just kept coming back, reminding Paul that he would never be free. He would always feel the cold, the rejection, and the complete absence of a mother's love. He would never understand it, but he would never be free of it. It didn't even piss him off anymore, just confused him.

Paul fell back to sleep, keeping the quilt tightly wrapped around him. He woke himself up snoring a couple of times. This always amused him. Next thing he knew, it was daylight outside, and he could smell freshly perked. He opened one eye and saw Murphy in the kitchen, standing over sizzling bacon, Barney drooling all over the place at his feet.

"You must have slept pretty good Paul," mused Murphy. "Heard you snoring to beat the band."

Paul said, "Yeah, I guess I was pretty tired."

Murphy then went on like the two of them had been sharing breakfast for years. "Hope you like your eggs scrambled, got some home fries too, and plenty of bacon. Don't believe all that shit they tell you about bacon. It tastes good because it is good. I really like to cook, learned how in the army. 'Course, my late wife wouldn't let me anywhere near the kitchen, 'cept toward the end when she got real sick with the cancer. Then she tried but just couldn't do it. Broke her heart, and mine too. I think women just need to feel useful. You know what I mean?"

Paul was listening, but it didn't seem to faze Murphy one way or the other. He just kept on talking. "Before I go to the cemetery for Barney's shitfest, I want to show you my shadowbox. I think you'll like it. And I kind of wanted to have a talk with you before we go to the cemetery 'cause it's crunch time. You can get your car keys anytime you want. Can't stop you from doing what you want to do. But I'm offering you to stay up here a while with me and Barney. Get yourself sorted out. Whaddya got to lose?"

By this time, the food was done, and *it tasted friggen delicious*, thought Paul. He also wondered out loud, "What the hell is a shadowbox, Murphy?"

Murphy said, "After your chow, Paul. I think you'll like it. Made it myself."

They ate noisily, no conversation now. Murphy was one of those eat with your mouth open, lip smacker kind of guys. Normally, this would have bothered the hell out of Paul, but this morning, it had no effect at all. It was as if Paul had gone through a crucible yesterday. He couldn't put his finger on it, but something was different. After all, here he was, sitting in a stranger's home, eating, going on as if he'd been here all his life. Paul was a planner, a detail-oriented guy. Sober, he wasn't much for spontaneity and certainly wasn't a believer in serendipity.

After breakfast, Paul washed up, shat, and rinsed his mouth out as best he could. Murphy was next door throwing another log on the fireplace in the trophy room. When he came back into the house, he asked, "Ready for the box?" They went into his bedroom, and Paul was looking at a 3-by-6-foot rectangular box, made of wood, shelved, with a background of—what else? —black velvet and a sliding glass door front. Inside was a treasure trove of memorabilia. What caught Paul's eye, instantly, was the faded ribbon holding the Silver Star. There were about seven other medals on either side of this, including the purple background cameo of George Washington on the Purple Heart award. He saw snippets of the faded citation for the Silver Star:

28 December 1944 ... In the Hurtgen forest ... despite having sustained wounds in the back, legs, and hand ... single-handedly attacked a fortified German machine gun position ... killed four and captured three of the enemy ... complete disregard for his own safety ... well-being of the men under his command ... Staff Sergeant Peter Murph ... refused transport to the rear until his wounded were cared for.

But there was more. A silver-framed photo of a young First Lieutenant and his beaming bride, his dress cap worn toward the back of his head, showing his curly hair. A chest full of medals, with a Combat Infantry Badge on top. A radiator cap from a Cadillac roadster. A trio of the Miraculous medal and the St. Christopher medal intertwined with a scapular of the Sacred Heart of Jesus. A faded picture of a young boy posing stiffly with an old man seated on a wooden chair. A matchbook cover advertising a correspondence course. A photo of Barney as a puppy. A newspaper clipping cutout of an obituary of his late wife, "Breda Murphy ... went into the arms of the Lord after a courageous battle with a long illness ... wife of Peter Murphy." A membership badge from the Better Business Bureau. A piece of a chewed-up dog toy. A gold wedding ring, matching the one on Murphy's left hand.

Paul could see Murphy's reflection as he was considering the case. Murphy was silent. Finally, he said, "Well, whaddya think? Made it myself. There's pretty much everything there in my life that means anything."

Paul turned around and inquired, "No kids? Didn't you and the Mrs. have any kids? Good Irish Catholic boy like you?"

Murphy laughed, "Did you see on that citation where it says I got shot in the legs? Well, it wasn't my legs. One of my balls got shot off, and I couldn't have any kids. I could still do my manly duties, though. Don't you worry about that. Hell, that's the main reason I looked so brave. I was really pissed off at those Hiney bastards. I didn't give a shit if they killed me or not. Hurt like hell. Naw, never had no kids, ... till now."

Paul said, "Man, I'm impressed. Hey, you think maybe you could make one for me.? I mean, I don't have all my medals and shit, but I could get copies and pictures of my kids, and my ex-wife, and my first taxicab and ... Kathy."

After a small pause, Murphy said, "Sure I could. I like the way you're thinking now, Paul. I like the way you're thinking."

Instantly, it came into focus what Murphy was saying. "I like the way you're thinking now." For the first time since meeting him, Paul said something that involved the future.

Murphy just pointed it out. Was it reflex? Or was Paul serious about getting a shadowbox? Something strange was going on.

"Come on, I've got the truck warming up for us. We had better get going before the damned snow starts again. Barney doesn't like to freeze his balls off on the seat, so you're gonna have to hold him in your lap." Paul thought that this act alone might cause him to relapse into suicidal thinking. Always the jokester, Paul was. He cracked himself right up.

On the way to the cemetery, Murphy started his "crunch time" conversation with, "Sometimes, after a good night's sleep, things seem a little clearer to us. You know what I mean, Paul? And sometimes a man gets an idea fixed in his head to the point where he doesn't see any other way to go. That's all I'm saying to you, Paul. Stick around a little bit, learn how to make some plaques. I'll even show you how to build your own shadowbox. I don't have enough work to hire you, and, in case you're interested, I'm not giving you back the dough you gave me yesterday, or the gloves. Figured I already earned that."

Paul responded, "Why, Murphy? Why should you even care what happens to me? I mean, unless you really meant that story you told me about you killing the old man."

Murphy just looked straight ahead at the road and said, "I meant that story and more. I'm not gonna be around much longer, that's clear. An old man can tell when another man is good or bad. You are a good man, Paul. You just don't know it yet. If you weren't, you wouldn't even be thinking about the crazy shit you're thinking about. That's clear to me too. Look, just give yourself a week, go into town. See where your girlfriend grew up and see if she picked up anything from this town that she brought to you. I think you'll learn more about yourself than her though. Just a hunch."

Paul was quiet. He looked over at the old man driving this piece of junk. Foul-smelling, bad-tempered dog sitting on his lap. With his scraggly white beard, ruddy complexion, tobacco-stained fingertips, and eyeglasses so thick that if he were to stare at anything too long, the object of his gaze would probably burst into flames. Willie Nelson on acid. Boxcar Willie after a bad night on the train. This guy was the epitome of cliché. But he had a certain dignity. An air of "say what you want, asshole, but I done it." Again, eyes and a face that looked lived in. To the max.

They pulled into the graveyard. Paul said, quietly, lightly touching Peter's shoulder, "Thanks, Murph, I'll think it over."

Barney farted.

Chapter 22

Blueprint for the Shadowbox

Paul had his keys in hand and immediately went to his rented car. It started right up. He didn't even think about opening the trunk, just letting the car idle while he went back to the grave of Kathryn Shanahan Urbanski. The gravesite had a strange familiarity about it now. The mystery of what it would look like and feel like was replaced by a going-to-church-like experience. He stood there watching, seeing Murphy in the distance, near Barney. The dog was looking for a new "-ski" site to bombard, per his innate, racist canine tradition. Paul stood over the grave, whispering, "What the hell is going on, Kathy? Who is this strange old man? He's put a damper on all my plans. I don't know what to do." He walked next door to Sheehy's gravesite, nodding in silent recognition.

He didn't feel alone, not at all, even though there was no living person in sight except that wack job Murphy. He felt rejuvenated by the crisp air. Looking up to the sky, he hoped for sundogs, but even Paul realized that maybe that was reaching too far.

Eventually, after an hour or so, Murphy and a newly cleansed Barney came walking back. Paul tried throwing a small stick to see if the dog would run for it. The dog looked at him like he was an asshole.

"I'm going down to the village for some coffee, Paul. Wanna come?" asked Murphy.

Paul replied, "I think I'll stick around a while. I've got some thinking to do."

If this statement bothered Murphy, he didn't show it in his demeanor.

"Suit yourself. When you're ready to come back to the house, just take a right outside the cemetery and go about seven miles till you see county road 258. Follow that road, and you'll find the house, no problem. I'm going to make some Irish stew. This is stew weather," said Murphy.

"Okay, I'll see you later," said Paul. Murphy had no conception what Paul was going to do next. Paul had even less vision.

After their departure, Paul sat on a bench that was near Kathy's grave. He was getting cold but still enjoying the solitude. By now, he should have been dead for twenty-four hours. Funny, his car was still here, so maybe they wouldn't have found his body yet. The blood and brain matter would have been frozen on top of the grave, possibly leaking and intermingling with Barney's ancient poop. Asses to ashes. The picture of this in his mind didn't bother him and certainly didn't scare him. He put his hands under his armpits, an old West Germany trick he often used when his paws were freezing, rocking back and forth unconsciously.

In his mind, he now saw a pretty girl, smiling that beautiful smile, in polka dot panties. He could hear her laugh, and it made him smile as well. Now he understood what Rest in Peace really meant. This was not a lonely place. It was quiet, even serene, but not lonely. No noise, no distraction. Welcoming. A goal. Paul thought about what to do next. He decided to write a note to Kathy.

I will always love you,

I will treasure our memories,

I will see you again,

It took some time, but you even got me to listen to and like Leonard Cohen,

And we will live forever in the Tower of Song.

On the ground, he found a small strip of electrical tape. He affixed the note to the back of the headstone with the tape. Picking up a small twig and leaf from the gravesite, he gently placed them on the car's front seat. It was only then he noticed the graves alongside hers. Like Murphy said, John Sheehy was on the right side of her and on the left was a headstone marked *Paul E. Shanahan 1922-1984* and *June H. 1926-*. Paul thought this was wondrous as she would not be alone here. The Spanish-War veteran and her dad would protect her and keep vigil. His face was red and wet from tears as he returned to the car.

His grum-bellies broke him from his stupor. He decided to eat. Paul thought, *These are good signs. I'm hungry, and I want to make the shadowbox. Maybe I will go back up to Murphy's house, just for another night. One more night can't hurt, can it?*

When he got back into the rental, which was still running, he found the car to be oven warm and almost out of gas. It was getting dark. Paul left the cemetery for the second time in as many days. Alive. Not well, but at least alive. At this point, anyway.

He re-fueled and got a coffee at the only open mini-mart gas station on the route back to the house. Their coffee was shit compared to the freshly perked.

The smoke was roaring out of both chimneys on his well-directed, and anxiously, but tacitly, awaited return. Barney strolled up, gave a half-assed excuse for a bark, and having fulfilled his watchdog responsibilities, went back to lay on the stairs. Paul looked for Murphy in the house, called out for him a couple of times. Murphy was next door, working with the jigsaw. He was slicing up a sheet of plywood into well-measured strips of various sizes.

"Hey Murph, let me give you a hand."

The woodsman asked, "You ever use a jig-saw"?

"Nope. How hard can it be?"

"Well, if you don't know what you're doing with a saw this size, and you fuck up, you won't have to worry about putting a slug into your brain-pan."

Paul took that as a not too subtle caveat.

"Just watch and learn, Paul," pontificated the old guy. "There's a lot to doing this right. Shit a computer can't do."

The slightly burnt smell of the wood and the dust flying, along with the smoky environs seemed other-worldly but comfortable to Paul. He heard Murphy say, "Figure out what we're gonna put in this thing. Only so much room, ya know. Just shit that you care about."

Paul thought, *it's only a couple of days, guess it couldn't hurt to leave a shadowbox behind. Not real sure about the black velvet thing though.* Murph set his jaw and was working *like a friggen watchmaker* on the wood.

Chapter 23

Summit at Painted Rock

Once the wood was cut and the pieces were laid out, Murphy explained how he was going to bevel the piece together. Interlocking pieces reinforced by glue. No nails or tacks. This was an important piece and was to be built like one. The whole damned thing is going to tell the story of a man's life. According to Murphy, "Only Jesus Christ was authorized nails in His story, and you certainly ain't Jesus."

They made their way over to the main house, and Paul smelled an enticing aroma. Irish stew. Sometimes known as Mulligan's stew or hobo stew. Just water, some beef bouillon cubes, carrots, potatoes, turnips, onion, and seared stew beef chunks. *Lotsa'* salt and pepper. The secret ingredient was a bottle of Guinness stout. Cook the ingredients over a low flame, covered, the longer, the better. Un-fuckup-able!

They sat over their bowls, all three of them. Barney had a little cold water added to his, and, quite indignantly, had to eat from his dish on the floor. He cast a menacing eye at Paul for this slight, but good manners prevailed. Paul had a lemonade, Murph a coffee, and both ate in silence. Well, as silent as a loud, open-mouthed eater and a slobbering canine could be. Didn't matter, the stew was delicious. Both men had two helpings, no more for the Barnster, but he was dozing next to the fireplace now. Murphy had made enough stew for the entire 3rd Armored Division. Leftovers would be welcomed for several days hence.

Sumptuous repast consumed, Murphy headed for bed. Paul headed for the couch and mothball-y quilt. After washing up, Paul stared at the fire in the way folks have stared at fires for centuries. Crackling, spitting, dancing, energy being consumed and produced simultaneously. It was fascinating. Different yet always the same.

They didn't have campfires in the projects where Paul grew up. They had steel trash barrel fires. A sort of pedestrian attempt at the bonhomie attached to the more traditional blazes. They were warm, but you had to keep the flying ashes from the burning newspapers under control, or you would torch the 'hood. Sometimes, one of the barrel-tenders had a transistor radio so you could listen to The Supremes' sing "Baby Love" and even dance to the "Bristol Stomp," which was even easier than "The Twist." Two steps back, two steps forward, kick, repeat.

Most of the time, fire or not, the kids just sat on the concrete steps and bull-shitted. If you were lucky, you had your arm around a local wench and brushed it against her tit a few times. If they didn't resist or move, you knew you were headed for a double or possibly a three-bagger night. This night, in the cozy cabin, it seemed to Paul that he missed those nights on the project's staircase. Poor kids, white and black, just chillin' and trying to get through the uncertainty of impending adulthood right around the corner. Like a lot of other impoverished kids in America, for the males, it was, "Do I wait to get drafted or do I join up? Army or Marines?" College was not an option. Never would you hear one of the homeboys say, "I think I've chosen Brown as my school." Especially not if your skin was the same color as that school's name. There was wit, though, street-smarts, false bravado, and unspoken empathy amongst the group. It just was the way it was.

Paul added a couple of split logs to the dying fire at Peter's house. He, for the first time in many years, remembered a time when he, Posie, and Bobby Ray had a three-way conversation. The memory came to him as vividly as if it were just happening at this moment.

The Army and Marines had a day or days when the entire primary training battalion did "service" work for the base. This was a day or week off from basic training, but not time off from work. Trainees were cattle carried to various sites on post, and a sergeant would yell out, "Five troops here." Move on to the next site. "Three asses here!" On this stop, the asses belonged to Posie, Bobby Ray, and Paul. They reported to a corporal who had to be at least fifty years old and was sorting through old field jackets. He was intense and nervous as he met them.

"My name is Corporal Jenkins, and you guys are to take this here bucket of paint and these three brushes and fill up this here wheel-barrow with these here rocks and take them up to that there path in front of the Tastee-Freeze. You will then place these rocks in a single line on both sides of that there path and then paint these here rocks white.

"It would behoove you boots not to jerk off on this detail because Sergeant First Class Yarboro is in charge, and he is a mean man. He used to be Captain Yarboro in Korea but to stay in the army and get his pension he had to take a bust to SFC, so he's not a happy camper, and he will rip off your heads and shit down your necks if you give him a chance. I don't fuck with him, you don't fuck with him, nobody fucks with him. Do I make myself clear?"

The three replied in unison, "Yes, corporal."

The first two loads of rocks were picked up and dumped on the path and laid out. Then the guys started painting. The subdued, contrary opinions emerged. Paul's was first.

"I hate the fucking army, this is stupid! Why the fuck are we painting fucking rocks! This is a waste of taxpayer money, and a waste of our time, and it's fucking stupid!"

Enter stage left, Bobby Ray. "We are painting these fucking rocks because SFC used to be Captain and Corporal older than shit said to paint these fucking rocks."

"Period."

"Orders is orders, and we are privates who get paid to obey orders."

Paul replied, "Oh yeah, well, what if we didn't paint these rocks? Would the fucking Tastee-Freeze collapse? Would the fucking war end? What in the fuck is the point?"

To his co-painter's surprise, Posie opined, "It's all in God's plan, you guys."

Bobby Ray hesitated, then said, "Posie, you a strange motherfucker, God's plan ... to paint fucking rocks?"

Posie just smiled and said softly—while painting, assiduously, "Yup, butterfly effect."

Then Paul got curious and asked, "What in the fuck are you talking about, Posie?" And then came the sermon on the mount. Well, on the slightly inclined path leading to one of the Tastee-Freezes on Fort Jackson. "If you put your paintbrush down for a minute to take a drink from your canteen and can't get the top back on right away, and you stand up and twist it harder until you finally get it right, you have changed your life, and mine and Bobby Ray's too. If we stop to look up at you to see what's going on, we have changed our behavior in, what seems to us, a minute way. We've altered each other's future in ways we can't see. What if it didn't happen and you just kept painting? Maybe the way you are holding your head, or sitting will affect the way you get up for chow. This conversation alone has changed all three of our lives in ways we can't tell, only God can. This conversation may make the difference whether we live or die in this war. Only God knows, and we are just part of his plan."

After a full minute of silence, Bobby Ray responded, "Posie, you had better get bare-assed naked, and get some cock 'cause you become feeble-minded as shit." Other than the fact that southern guys called "pussy" cock, Paul thought this was a good, if not elegant, summation. At the time.

Now, lying on this couch, staring into the fire, Paul thought about what Posie had said. *Man, that's some deep shit.* Posie knew he was going to die. He was just following God's plan for him. He had already accepted that fact of his life. Willingly. Predestination some might call it, but Posie was okay with it. Is that any different from what Paul was attempting to do right now? *I think this might be what Bobby Ray might have been thinking when he stared off into the tree line, beer in hand, ass in wheelchair.* Did that conversation in front of the Tastee-Freeze cause Murphy to appear in the graveyard, at that time, in that specific spot? Or was Paul just mind-fucking himself again? He didn't remember falling asleep, and the devils did not visit him on that night.

Chapter 24

Filling the
Shadowbox

Paul woke, alone, no Peter, no Barney. Just an empty bowl and a box of Captain Crunch on the kitchen table. He sat down to breakfast and remembered that he hadn't called his ex-wife, kids, or anyone else back in Albany, in over ten days. This was the norm for Paul, however. No one was alarmed or surprised as he wasn't much of a telephone guy. It wasn't mean-spirited. It was just the way he was. He called her. Chit-chatted a little, "How're the kids," etcetera. She asked where he was and when he was going to be back in town. He said, "I'm not sure, probably pretty soon." She did say, "I wish you'd call more often, we do worry." He assured her he would try.

He went looking for Peter and found some tracks in the snow leading to the work shed. Two shuffling human prints and multi-dog tracks with a penis line in the snow nearly bisecting those tracks. On entering, Paul was hit with the, by now, familiar smells of woodcuts, smoke, and glue. It was enticing. On the far shelf, he could see his completed shadowbox. It was drying from the last coat of shellac, the back wall of the box lined with black velvet. It was *friggen awesome*. Especially with the black velvet!

Murphy said, "She's about done now. The hard part comes next, and it's all on your head. You gotta figure out what goes in there." Paul immediately started his mental inventory. He wasn't at all sure what to place in there to represent his life. It was clear to him though, he had to fill it with stuff that was important to himself, only himself or it was meaningless. The old man suggested that Paul make paper patterns, in actual size, to get an idea of space, room, and motif. "What I'd do," he said, "is make paper cut outs to be sure the shit fits."

Paul replied, "Good idea." At which Murphy cautioned, "This is going to take some time. It's your shit. What's important to you. Make it like you're gonna show this to God as your passport to get your ass into heaven. Don't fuck it up." Peter gave him a couple of old cardboard boxes, flattened out and a pair of shears.

"Here, use this as your dummy stuff."

Murphy and Barney left Paul alone in the shed. Paul started to think about what was going into his box. *Keep it simple, stupid,* thought Paul, *stuff that matters to your life.* No one will know what every piece means, just like no one knows every piece of another person's life is or what those pieces totaled up to in the form of human existence. Passport to heaven … *more like a trip ticket through hell,* mused Paul. Tactile Purgatory.

Excitedly, he started by laying out the cardboard and hammering it flat to make it easier to write on with the ancient ballpoint pen. He knew he wouldn't have any of the real stuff here, but he could retrieve a good portion of it back at his home in Albany. In his past, he was a little bit of a sentimentalist hoarder in that respect. He had a couple of boxes up in the attic over the garage where he kept his stash. Whoa, Paul reflected with amusement more than shock. *Did I just say when I get back to Albany? Did Murphy mind fuck me with this project? Oh well, if I don't go back and I leave the cut-outs in the box, someone could fill it with the real deal when they figure it all out. Maybe my son could do it.* So, he began the cut-outs. And to make sure that a rationale was assigned to each, he wrote a postscript on individual pieces.

His City of Albany Livery and Chauffeur License. Even though he probably picked up fewer passengers and ran more hookers than any cab driver in history, 'cept for Welch. It merited a spot. Army medals: His Combat Infantry Badge—CIB, Bronze Star Medal with V device, National Defense Service Medal, Sharpshooter M-14, Expert M-16 badges, Parachutists Badge, and Good Conduct Medal. The only ones Paul felt good about and had earned were the Sharpshooter and Parachutist badges, the rest was gravy. Even though the CIB was the most widely admired by your peers, Paul felt that by just being "in country" he didn't deserve it. Same with the Bronze Star. Almost everyone in that company got at least that. Most guys earned it. Paul never felt he did anything to deserve it.

Photograph of Kathy. He wondered if his ex-wife would take offense or be hurt by this but rationalized that this was *his* shadowbox and was telling *his* story. So, the pic goes in. It was an old Instamatic of Kathy standing in front of her brand new '69 Mustang. Her with the miniskirt and legs to die for and a smile more radiant than the damned car's grill. The photo was worn out, but the old beer tears shed onto the picture didn't ruin the image.

Schaffer beer can pull tabs and bottle caps. *Yes,* thought Paul, *for posterity someone should know that some folks did drink Schaffer's beer.*

Lineman and cable splicer's knife. This tool was the Leatherman of its generation. Paul's was left with only one side still covered in wood and a couple of dings on the blade, but he never needed a replacement knife in his lineman duties.

Taxi Medallion. Unlike the individual hack license, this metal orb indicated ownership and proof of insurance for the vehicle and that Paul owned a lot of cabs. The folks in the know would realize just how politically powerful one was who possessed this disc. He would pin this disc onto the certificate from the Mayor of the City of Albany thanking him for being one of the City's best employers.

He added a 1" by 2" tin, old country Irish bubble gum container holding an emerald stick pin with emerald cuff links. A gift from his dad, who got it from his dad, who got it from his dad. He figured that if his son wanted it, which he hoped he did, he could take it from the box.

Paul needed a break as he was hungry, tired, and excited at the same time. Looks like at least one more night on the couch, with fresh perked and Cap'n Crunch in the A.M.

He entered the main house where he heard Murphy snoring and his useless piece of caninity sleeping in front of the fireplace. The dog didn't even bat an eye or wag a tail on his arrival. Or, thankfully, even fart.

Chapter 25

Die Teufel kommen in die Nacht

He threw a couple of small pieces of wood on the fire, replaced the screen, shed his trousers, took a piss, and got ready for some sleep. Usually, falling asleep was hard for Paul. He envied folks who could just lay their heads back and fall asleep anywhere, anytime. This supposedly "quiet" time was almost torture for him.

He reflected on a gasthaus in Dachau, called Willi's. That's what his buddies called the place because the owner was named Willi, and the correct name for the place was, in the typical German lexicon, impossible to pronounce without buying a friggen vowel or two. Willi was a good guy. His English was so-so, and his main fear was that the G.I.'s would try to rape his sixteen-year-old daughter, who did part-time service there as a waitress. She weighed about 120, which wouldn't be bad if it were pounds, but it was kilograms. All five feet of her.

Even with drunken soldiers, Willi's fears were for naught. She had to have the biggest tits in West Germany, and Paul was a tit man. But Paul had standards. Incredibly low standards, but they existed. And Paul considered Willi a friend. She was, by far, the safest sixteen-year-old girl in the Village of Dachau, West Germany.

Willi's story was compelling. In *double u double u deuce*, the big one, he was a tanker in the SS Panzer Division

Totenkopf, Death's Head, a notorious unit to say the least. He claims to have never participated in pogroms or wiping out villages, but on the way to getting to know him better, Paul had his doubts about that part of his story. Willi was sent back to Germany from the Eastern front because of frostbite. This was easily verifiable because Willi was prone to removing his shoes and socks when he was in his cups and show you both feet with a grand total of two toes. The pinky toe and next-door neighbor on his left foot. He also has only four fingers on his left hand. He said he was lucky. And maybe he was. At least he still had his nose.

One night, Willi was drunk. He loved to play his accordion for the boys and was pretty good at it. However, he seemed to know only one American song. Red River Valley, always Red River Valley. His buxom offspring would sing the words in English. Even when drunk, the song got old quickly. Paul was the lone American in the bar that night, and Willi came over and sat with him. He knew that Paul had gotten his orders for Viet Nam and this was kind of a farewell party. Willi showed Paul a photograph of a sixteen-year-old kid in a black uniform. The picture was that of Willi. He put his arm around Paul's shoulder and slurred, "Mein Freund, Die Teufel kommen in die Nacht." *The devils come in the night.* He was spot on.

Wiped out now, Paul slept. If they hooked him up to a rapid eye movement machine, he'd have burnt the motor out. *Here they come,* a man with no legs arguing with a man with no nose over snakes that were on fire all around them. And then it was so cold, so terribly frigid, and Paul knew he was locked out of his house again tonight and couldn't find an open boiler room to warm up in. His sneakers and socks, both wholly holey, encased his shivering blue feet. Bobby Ray kept singing "Folsom Prison Blues," while waving his .45 Colt pistol around his head. Three black guys in Panther regalia were taking Kathy into a bedroom to have their way with her. Paul tried to fight, but his arms would not move, and Kathy kept saying, "It's okay, Paul. We have to do what we can to make up for all our years of enslaving these people." But she didn't say this with words she said it with a look. And Paul understood. The potters didn't have the right, but the Panthers did. And then Welch Green would appear in his pimp uniform and shake his head, knowingly. Bobby Ray's leg and arm were on display in a meat market counter along with Jack Palito's brains, and a nose from some guy as well as four fingers and eight toes. And they were lined up very neatly, and no one seemed to pay them any mind. Billy Flynn cried "nazdrovia," and Paul, still paralyzed, couldn't get out of this horrible place. And then Murphy was shaking him, and he was back. "It's okay, Fogarty, it's all right."

It wasn't all right, though.

Die Teufel kommen in die Nacht. Every fucking night.

Chapter 26

The Shadowbox Time Paradox

After a cup of freshly perked, Paul took his first shower in a few days. It was a rusty ass shower stall made of white sheet metal with a couple of rivets popped, but the weak stream was warm, and the Ivory soap bar was only half worn down. Murphy was absent, *probably walking Barney*, thought Paul. He wondered what Murph's life would be like—now that his wife was dead—without the mutt. Hard to say. Time to get back to the wood.

He looked at his cutouts so far and had to wrap his mind around where he left off. This was easy enough, but his mind went off on a little tangent, as it was often wont to do. Here he was, filling a shadowbox, a time capsule for sure, and it seemed to him that time was standing still. He was in a state of suspended mental animation. No thoughts of suicide, tomorrow, or *is it cold outside? Or hot? Or light enough?* Just yesterdays, in cardboard, to be placed on black velvet. When it's done, he wondered if it will be a time vacuum. Will anyone even look at it? Or care? Back to work.

A chestnut on a shoestring. Paul could probably dig around in the snow later and find one. If he did find a chestnut, he would have to drive a hole through the center and place a knotted shoestring through the nut. When he was a kid, there were a lot of secret processes one could use to make your nut harder. Some guys put them in the freezer.

Others swore by shellac or vinegar soaking. The whole idea was to swing your hanging nut at another guy's hanging nut, and the one that broke first was the loser. Every time you won, you tied a knot in your hang string, like a notch on a gunfighter's pistol handle. Kind of like who's got the biggest cock contest but projects style.

The next entry was already in his possession. It was a scapular given to him by Posie at Fort Benning, in 1967. A scapular was a flattened cloth religious icon, usually with a stencil of Jesus, showing you His Sacred Heart with little quotation marks around his head to show he was holy. The back was either a short prayer or a stencil of the Blessed Virgin Mary, Mother of God. It was designed to drape around your neck with a green string, and it was said to have been blessed by one authorized to sanctify these totems.

Some guys carried condoms in their wallets. Paul carried the scapular. It was faded and beat up, but it was still important to him. At first, Paul thought taking it might be a no go because Posie was a Seventh Day Adventist but figured a guy in good with God wouldn't be involved in a heresy-type situation. He wondered whether Posie or Bobby Ray or Jack was wearing one when they became bloodied in the bush. He could be pretty sure that Posie was, not so much the others.

He remembered the Instamatic color photo of himself and Bobby Ray posing at Fort Jackson in AIT—Advanced Individual Training—Radio Operator School. They were both in the ready, front bayonet position with their M-14 rifles and unscabbarded bayonets peering menacingly, growling at the camera operator. Both thought they were hot shit because they were acting corporals after basic and got to wear an armband with two stripes on their left arms. With their helmet liners and fake stripes and newish green fatigues, they just looked like two kids playing war. Which was, in fact, exactly what they were.

Paul knew a beer mug would never fit into this box, and he had a tremendous collection of beer mugs from all over the world at home. He also had some beer coasters from West Germany. His best one, even though he knew it was beer-stained, was a Hofbräuhaus souvenir from the Oktoberfest in Munich, 1967. An unbelievable, crazy wet dream for a nineteen-year-old alcoholic soldier. He had another coaster from Willi's in Dachau, which he would insert in the box backward. The reason for this was because, in still-readable ink was a name—Marta Stang, written in Paul's handwriting. Paul had no idea who this person was or why he had written the name but figured it was a pretty good indicator of his mental state at the time. He never intended to solve the mystery, not wanting to find if he had done even more evil in his life. But it would be posted in the box as an oxymoronic memento of things not remembered.

Murphy entered, glanced at Paul, and declared his intention to defecate. Barney having already bombed his daily crypts. Paul kept working as if this was the most natural thing in the world with no hint of irony.

He knew that he had stashed at home a protractor, for measuring distance on maps, ranger beads, for figuring out how far he had walked in the jungle, and a P-38, a little tin can opener for C rations that could slide on your dog tags. The protractor was barely readable any more after being exposed to jungle rot and years of sitting in a box, but Paul still knew how to work it over a map. He was sure he could still call in an artillery strike if need be but wasn't seeing that happening soon. Ranger beads almost looked like a little rosary. Every time a tall soldier's left foot hit the ground fifty-five times, you moved a bead up—Paul was tall. When you got to your ten beads, you moved a big bead up. You had just walked a kilometer. After about five kilometers, you relocated your position on your map and started all over again. Poor man's GPS. Posie suggested to Paul that he could use it as a rosary, but he never did. And the P-38, after fifty years, could still open any can easily. These three items would take up little room in the box, but were, on reflection, an essential portion of Paul's past.

He knew that he would have to pick up a small package of tomato plant seeds. If no one else understood why this item was placed in here, he was sure Packy would. There was a ticket stub from 1964, Hawkins Stadium, Menands, New York, for a concert starring James Brown and the Famous Flames, Patti LaBelle and the Bluebells, Bobby "Blue" Bland and Joe Tex. *Pretty "colorful" lineup*, he thought. It kind of reminded him of the red suit he owned, but that's long gone and would be too big for the box. That was a good thing.

In the top center, he placed cutouts of the rubbings of John Palito and David Michael Posie, taken from the Viet Nam Memorial wall in D.C. Right under that, he put a 173rd Airborne red, white, and blue shoulder patch.

One of the only real items that he knew he had placed in a left-center position. His thinking was that left-center was the location of the human heart. It was Kathy's library signature card, last date March 8, 1960, that he had taken from her high school to this place. He didn't want to stick tacks into the card as if it would hurt her. After some thought, he placed one in each upper corner and only one tack in the middle bottom. With the strands of hair, he had snagged from her mother's house tucked into the top. Kathy's stigmata, or so it felt to Paul.

His final addition would be beer checks from Ziggy's, which he would sprinkle throughout the box, glued in the empty spaces, like beery stars in the dark sky of black velvet.

He was done. Or was he just starting?

Chapter 27

The Death of Paul Fogarty

Fogarty waited all afternoon for Murph to come and check on his work, but he was nowhere to be seen. He went over to the main house to check on his new-found amigo and saw Murph sitting in an overstuffed chair just looking at the flames.

Paul said, "I'm finished with it, Murph. Want to come and look"?

Peter answered, "I'm sure it's fine. It's yours anyway, not for me to say one way or the other."

It was clear to Paul now that he would have to go back to Albany to get the items he needed for the shadowbox. He should see his kids too before he made the trip back up here. It would probably only take a couple of days to get the items he needed and then come back up and finish the box for good. And, he thought, *what better statement could I make about my life than that rectangular piece of wood?* Murph and Barney were both dozing by the fireside. Paul ate some re-heated stew and decided on an early quit for the night.

Devils made no appearance on this night.

It was a little after eight in the morning when Paul woke. The house was cozy, warm, and empty. He figured where Murph was. He'd be at the cemetery right now, looking for a gravestone ending in a vowel for his xenophobic dog. Paul went over to the shed to put the finishing touches on his new masterpiece.

The shadowbox was moved a little to the left of where Paul had placed it yesterday. He figured, correctly, that Murph had come in to look at it. And knowing Murph, even for this short period, he was sure that he inspected the back of the piece as critically as the front. Paul was proud of his handiwork and was eager to get back to Albany for the real articles to place in the box. He decided that tomorrow was the day to go back home. Sooner the better. When the project was finished, he would decide what to do with it when he returned to Cattaraugus. Maybe he could just leave it with Murph to be forwarded to his heirs. He decided to find Peter and tell him about his plan.

Paul drove to the cemetery on this cold, drizzly gray day. *A Germany day for shit-sure*, thought Paul. He saw Peter's rust-bucket of a truck haphazardly abandoned inside the gate. Murph's version of parking rules was not germane to civilization elsewhere. This cemetery had three cascading levels, the highest being in the front, separated by bushes for each field. It was like three separate graveyards. Peter and Barney were not on level one, so Paul drove down to level two. There was a car running, with someone inside, but it wasn't the curmudgeon or the canine. Paul parked and decided to walk down to level three. Level three was where Kathy was, as well as old man Sheehy. Paul figured he could visit the grave as long as he was here and explain to Kathy's dirt his reasoning for the delay in their communion.

He didn't get far before he saw Barney. The mutt was just slowly wandering over the graves. Not sniffing or shitting or anything. The dog looked lost. Where the hell was the old guy?

Then he saw the body ... or rather the clothes that covered it. It was Murph. Frozen solid, blue, eyes open, and mouth in a sort of semi-smile, he was lying on Sheehy's grave, right next to Kathy's. He was all in.

Paul sat next to Murph's mortal remains and made a tiny cross on the dead man's forehead with his thumb. He felt a tear run down his cheek, and it froze immediately. Quietly, he sobbed.

Paul called 911, reported in, and awaited the police. Barney came and sat next to him, not even looking at his old master's remains.

The police and EMS came. The paramedic checked the body and radioed a code for dead at the scene, beyond resuscitation. He ran an EKG strip in three different views, all flat line, tore them in half, and gave the halves to the police officer, clipping the remaining halves to his patient care report. The officer questioned Paul about the discovery. He asked if Paul knew the man lying there. Paul said, "I've only known him for three days. He put me up at his house. We met in this cemetery and became friends. I know how weird that sounds. I'm still confused about the whole thing." The officer raised an eye with a new interest in the circumstances of this unattended death. In the course of about twenty-five minutes, Paul told his tale.

The officer, now dubious, but appearing neutral, asked Paul to open the trunk on the rental car. Paul and the officer peered into the trunk and there lay the unused, new shotgun. The cop lifted it, inspected it, and replaced it back into the trunk. He shook his head and said simply, "Wow. Okay, I'll make out the report, and I'd like you to come down to the station to record a statement. At your soonest convenience, if that's okay with you."

Paul said, "Sure, can you call a tow truck and have his truck towed to his house?" The officer knew precisely where Peter's abode was and said, "No problem."

Paul said, "I'll take the dog with me if that's okay with you. I'll take care of it."

The officer nodded, secretly glad that he didn't have to make out a stray animal report.

Paul asked, "Is it okay if I take the dog back to the house and then come down to the station?" The man in blue agreed and thanked Paul for his help in this matter.

Chapter 28

The Resurrection

The next few days were a whirlwind of actions and reactions for Paul. After filling out the police report, which was surprisingly routine and facile, he talked to the coroner. The death doc told Paul an autopsy was in order as Murph had died alone and after the remains thawed out, the heart attack or stroke should be confirmed. Paul said, "Okay, but it's not my call."

The coroner said, "Well, we can't find any next of kin, so after the post, we'll have to put him on ice until we can dispose of the remains."

"I don't think he had any kin," replied Paul. "I mean, he didn't mention anyone, but I only knew him for a short time. His wife died a while ago."

The MD said, "I know, I'm also an undertaker and did her services. I don't remember any relatives coming to that one either, except for Peter."

Paul left the police station and pondered this new dilemma. He decided to contact a local lawyer and see if he could get a decision on the disposition of Peter's body. The lawyer, a local guy named Flynn, was a great help. He said they would do an official search for next of kin, and, if there were no answers in a reasonable amount of time, a probate judge could make those final disbursement decisions. Paul also got a temporary permit to live in Peter's house while the search was going on as he was committed to taking care of Barney, who adjusted to this arrangement remarkably well.

After three weeks, Flynn contacted Paul. "No relatives found. No will either. Are you okay with having the remains cremated?"

Paul reflexively replied, "Okay, but I think we should have some kind of service, right?" Lawyer Flynn agreed.

The next day, Paul, in Murph's truck with Barney by his side, drove to the funeral home and crematorium. The Priest was brief, the burn was quick, and the urn was transported by hearse to the cemetery where all this drama started. He was buried in Section two, next to Mrs. Murphy. Barney, respectfully, stayed in the truck, holding his defecator urges well. Paul prayed his triad of prayers and a good Act of Contrition for this heroic friend.

After the burial, Paul drove back to the house, fired up both stoves, and fed Barney. He phoned the car rental agency for a reservation for the next day to go to Albany to receive his totems for his shadowbox. Paul made it a week-long, figuring it might take that long to gather up the mementos and return. The house and "estate" were now under probate, but it looked like it was going to end up in Paul's hands. He wondered if Cattaraugus could use a new taxi company.

On the way back to his birthplace, Paul saw the most brilliant set of sundogs ever. Barney yawned. *God bless.*

Daniel A. Doherty

Dan is from Albany, New York. He's had a varied career path including serving for thirty-three years on the Albany Fire Department, retiring as a Captain/Paramedic. Dan served in the US Army and Army Reserve for fourteen-years. He is currently a Warrant Officer in the South Carolina State Guard, and has been a full-time faculty member at Hudson Valley Community College in Troy, New York, as well as Lead Instructor at State University of New York at Cobleskill in their respective paramedic programs.

From 2010 to 2011 Dan served as a paramedic for the Saudi Red Crescent Authority in Riyadh, Kingdom of Saudi Arabia. He is an avid runner and has completed over 100 marathons and ultra-marathons. This is his first novel. He now resides near Myrtle Beach, South Carolina with his wife.

Book Club Questions

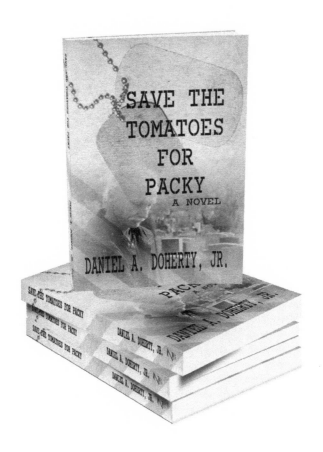

1. What is the significance of theme of sundogs appearing throughout the book?

2. In Chapter 4, you referred to the term "wreckese" that the long term, alcoholic bar patrons used as a separate language. Can you elaborate on the reception and transmission of this perceived phenomenon?

3. It is ironic that in Chapter 6 -Bloods, the life of Bobby Ray, the racist, was saved by two black soldiers. Was this your intention? And did Bobby Ray ever realize who saved him, even though he was unconscious? (Part of my answer will be, in combat, as opposed to the rear, there are only light green and dark green soldiers).

4. Did you intend to present Kathy's illness and Paul's alcoholism as potentially, concurrent fatal diseases in progression?

5. In Chapter 10, did Paul's taking of Kathy's old library card from the high school, and a lock of her hair from her mother's house unconsciously trigger his positive reception to Peter's idea of building a shadowbox as remembrance?

6. Why are the sporadic references to Paul's abusive childhood not developed more? (Answer, I wanted to indicate that as he got older, when he was presented with his myriad of life problems, he was even more vulnerable than the average man because of a lack of any kind of nurturing relationship in childhood).

7. Was the assault on Steve, the bar owner, a cry for help from Bobby Ray? Was his history of disruptive behavior a sign that it was going to get worse in time?

8. Why was Barney, Peter's dog given a character position in the book? Was the dog used as a means of continuum for Paul's fate or just curmudgeonly comic relief?

9. In the Chapter 23 -Summit at Painted Rock was Posie representing Jesus' sermon on the mount? Was he aware of his impending doom, as was Christ?

10. Would you like Paul to return to Cattaraugus to live out his days?

A Note from the Publisher

Dear Reader,

Thank you for reading Daniel A. Doherty's first novel, *Save the Tomatoes for Packy*.

We feel the best way to show appreciation for an author is by leaving a review. You may do so on any of the following sites:

www.ZimbellHousePublishing.com
Goodreads.com
or your favorite retailer

⊰⊱⊰⊱

Join our mailing list to receive updates on new releases, discounts, bonus content, and other great books from
Daniel A. Doherty
and

Or visit us online to sign up
http://www.ZimbellHousePublishing.com